681 Beverly Drive
Lake Wales, Fl. 33853
1-877-676-2285



ISBN-13: 978-0-9798351-8-6
ISBN-10: 0-9798351-8-6

Printed in the United States of America

# The Valley
# of
# Shadows and Shame

by

Dianne Lininger

A special thanks to Shane and Kathy Glover for allowing illustrator April Sampson to use the likeness of their beautiful daughter Shannon, as the cover model for Abby.

~ Dianne
Lininger

# Preface

During the midst of a massacre, fifteen year old Abigail Colter is rescued by the Cavalry after a year of brutal captivity by renegade Apaches.

The traumatized Abby attempts to resume normal life in post Civil War Texas. Unfortunately, she becomes the anathema of her small town of Wildwillow after it becomes known she was a squaw to the notorious and violent Chief Raging Storm. Soon, greater degradation ensues as the ultimate shame befalls her.

A devout Christian, Abby is now forced to confront the cruelty and hypocrisy of so-called God-fearing, decent folk wherever she travels throughout the old west.

Through the passing years, her rationale transforms as her faith wanes. Gradually, the once true believer drifts into a life enveloped by remorseless lawlessness with all its ramifications and consequences.

# Chapter One

The early spring night was a dark one with no moon and few stars. An unnatural stillness and prevailing tension filled the air. The scattered crowd appeared anxious and uneasy. Gradually a disturbing sound began to swell in their ears; a rapid thumping resembling a wildly beating desperate heart. A distant horse's swift hoof beats were drawing ever nearer.

Soon a familiar figure emerged out of the crisp darkness. A sweaty rider waved his broad-brimmed hat high above him. "Chief Raging Storm is dead!" he cried out repeatedly.

The rider pulled his horse to an abrupt stop, directly before the stage depot near the town square. "They massacred the entire renegade tribe near the river in Bone Canyon!" he shouted as the curious crowd quickly closed in. "They found Abby!" He whooped jubilantly, waving his hat high again. "Abby is alive!"

"Praise the almighty above!" exclaimed a worn-looking, stout woman in a faded calico dress. Instantly, she fell to her knees in the dirt street as she wept joyously into her loosely woven shawl.

A natty stranger in a bowler hurried to her side. He smelled of pungent cologne. Solicitously, the gentleman extended his hand.

Through her joyful sobs, the woman grasped his smooth hand and slowly rose. Her eyes glistened with relief and exultation.

"They rescued my daughter," she said with a trembling smile. "We feared her dead for well over a year now. We heard the cavalry was closing in on those renegades. My Henry said it was false hope that brought me here. But I prayed to the Lord!"

"Obviously prayers are answered for the truly devout, dear lady," the dapper gentleman replied.

The woman closed her eyes and took a deep, contented breath.

"My Abby's coming home. I never gave up faith. I was away visiting my sister Eudora over in Sweetwater when the Apaches raided our place. I should have forced Abby to come along." She clenched her fists tightly.

"All will be well again," the gentleman reassured her.

"Yes, Abigail is a survivor." She beamed with pride. "My name is Martha Colter."

"I am Howard Juliuson of Fredericksburg, Virginia. I was visiting distant relations on my way to San Francisco. This has been my final day in Wildwillow."

The Colter woman quickly turned away and stared hopefully into the vast, empty darkness beyond town. Her demeanor suddenly became tense and grievous.

"My poor Abby," she whispered. "What an ordeal my girl must have endured."

"A decent Christian woman would have killed herself before falling amidst the clutches of near-naked heathen savages," drawled one rawboned woman to another as she glanced at Martha Colter with disdain.

"How dare you!" Mrs. Colter snapped. "Abby is just a child. She turned fifteen only last month!" Martha shook as she tightened her loosely woven shawl.

"Look a'yonder!" a small boy shouted suddenly.

Emerging in the distance was a long, winding, fiery, blue dust cloud.

"It's the cavalry!" someone screamed. "The cavalry is coming!"

Soon they rode into full view, their torches held high. The column of pony soldiers paraded down the wide street between rows of rectangular, two-story wooden buildings. The weary men were haggard and unshaven. They appeared to be more an army of defeat than of victory. The smell of livestock combined with the smoke from the torches and the sweat from the men mingled with the fragrant spring air to form a haunting stench.

Half-way down the long line of soldiers, a young woman sat bareback astride a pinto stallion. She was clad entirely in buckskins. Her long, yellow hair fell loosely about her back and shoulders and reached below her waist. The startled silence suddenly gave way to loud gasps.

"Look at her! She should be ashamed coming back like that!" said a contemptuous woman's voice from the back of the crowd.

"The girl's probably more savage than civilized by now," remarked a masculine voice Martha recognized as Benton Foss, the tailor. "The Apaches do that to captives in no time."

"Everyone knows what those vile savages do to women!" exclaimed old lady Grady. "She should have never returned at all."

Burning tears streaked down Mrs. Colter's face.

"Abby!" she shrieked, as she raced with outstretched arms to reclaim her near-lost daughter.

The girl did not respond. She merely sat, numbly catatonic upon the horse. Her gaze was directed firmly ahead, never once displaying a sideways glance.

"Abby!" Martha Colter screamed again, as she grasped the fringe of the young girl's buckskins. "Abby! Stop!" The mother dashed forward and seized the horse's rope. "Abby! Abby!"

No reply ensued. Abby remained in a daze, her body as still and her eyes as vacant as a soulless cadaver.

"What's wrong with her?" Martha shrieked to a passing soldier.

The lanky, hollow-eyed man appeared irritated. Wearily, he dismounted. Without a word he roughly pulled Abby down from the horse.

Weeping, Martha Colter flung her shaky arms about her daughter.

"You're home now, Abby. You're home!" Her trembling fingers stroked the young girl's uncombed hair.

Abby's body started to quiver. Her dazed eyes began to blink and her lips and chin trembled. An expression of disbelief came over her face.

"Mama?" she murmured.

"Yes child, oh yes!" Mother squealed in delight. She led her daughter away from the Indian pony toward the waiting buckboard.

During the journey home Abby sat with her feet upon the seat and her arms wrapped around her knees. She frequently rocked back and forth. Owls screeched in the late darkness and coyotes howled mournfully in the distance. Often, Abby shuddered or gasped. Her body remained rigid and tense.

"It's all right child. You're safe," Mother constantly reassured her.

"Those are Indian sounds, Mama!"

"No Abby, not anymore. It's over now. Calm yourself."

"I wish I had died!" Abby cried out in a burst of bitter tears.

"No! No, child. God allows even terrible things to happen for a reason. Some good will come of this. Be patient and have faith."

"A part of who I am has died, Mama. I don't feel the same anymore."

"We've all changed through this ordeal. It's only going to make us stronger. It's part of God's plan."

"How is Papa? I saw an arrow, a flaming one, strike his arm before the Apaches seized me. Is he all right?"

Martha swallowed deeply before she spoke.

"We haven't been able to plant as much corn as we used to. The arrow hit an upper muscle. The plowing is too painful. It's been a pure hardship. I do what I can, but it's not enough."

"I fear Papa won't have me back," Abby said dejectedly. She began to sob.

"Now what kind of addled reasoning is that? You're our blood! Why you're coming home will be better for him than any fancy Philadelphia doctor's concoction."

"You could never imagine what happened, Mama." Abby's jaw trembled as she spoke.

"No, but Colters stand by our kinfolk. You remember that!"

An awkward silence prevailed the remainder of the journey. At last, through the darkness, their farm came into view.

"Is that our place?" Abby exclaimed in disbelief as she started to rise in the buckboard.

"Almost half the farm burned down before our neighbors and a few townsfolk came to the rescue," Mother explained. "They were kind enough to help us rebuild, too. But everything was put together differently this time. More practical, they said."

"More boxy, I'd say. Looks like a completely different farm."

"We lost most of our livestock to the Apaches as well."

"Yes, I remember," Abby said with lowered eyes.

"Look, a light's burning. Henry must still be up! I'll unhitch the horses later. First, I want to see his expression." Martha beamed with elation.

With trepidation, Abby cautiously entered the changed structure that used to be her home. The sparse, unfamiliar interior possessed a strange grimness.

The light of a lantern revealed the outline of a man half-seated, half-sprawled across a heavy, wooden table.

"Henry," Martha whispered. "Henry, wake up!" She nudged her husband softly.

Moaning, he opened his bleary eyes and groggily sat up. His gaze now fell directly on Abby. Abruptly he arose. His body shaking, he reached hastily for the lantern and held it out before him.

Abby was dismayed at how greatly he had aged in such a brief span of time. His hair appeared thinner and grayer. His face was more deeply furrowed. Also he carried himself differently. He seemed more flaccid and stoop-shouldered.

His countenance, upon first viewing her, unnerved Abby. His stare appeared to be one of horror and disbelief as though she had become disfigured, or ruined.

His face twisted and tears fell from his blood-shot eyes as he choked to speak. "Abby," he moaned. "Abby!" He hurried to welcome her. Abby rushed into his embrace.

The large feather bed in which she slept felt strangely uncomfortable now. Abby roamed the small house in darkness trying to remember the way everything used to be. She built a fire in the hearth. Teeth clenched, she fought back tears as she gathered up her discarded buckskins and tossed them into the flames. Through the east window she watched the sun slowly rise over the rocky hills beyond.

"Abby!" Mother gasped as she emerged from an adjoining room. "What is that dreadful stench?"

"Memories, bad memories. I couldn't sleep, Mama. The harder I tried, the more I was unable."

"Sit down. We can chat while I prepare the biscuits and eggs."

"You don't have to wait on me, I'm not a guest."

"Chores can wait awhile. You need to rest, and get accustomed to the place again."

"No, I need to get busy with my old routine, as soon as possible."

"You can feed the chickens, and clean the coop," declared her father as he stepped forward, buttoning his faded blue cotton shirt.

"Martha smiled warmly. "If you feel up to it, maybe later you can help me in the garden with the squash and beans."

"It's comforting to find some of my dresses salvaged," Abby enthused. "Guess Grandma's old trunk must be indestructible."

"I feared you might have outgrown those things," Mother replied. "However, you do appear mighty thin."

Abby's mouth twitched. Involuntarily, she wrinkled her nose. "Meals consisting of beaver, foxes, raccoons, and prairie dogs were not exactly delectable." She shuddered. "However, the mescal roots were at least palatable. I used to cook them inside holes covered with grass and leaves, topped with sand. They tasted tough, but were also quite sweet."

Henry Colter bolted upright! Jaw tight, he clenched his hands as he glared belligerently down at his startled daughter. Abruptly, he turned and departed the house.

Stunned and bewildered, Abby looked up at her mother.

"Did I say something offensive?"

Martha frowned, and sat down beside her. She wrapped an affectionate arm around Abby's shoulders.

"Papa doesn't like thinking about you in the hands of the Apaches. Remember what they did to your brother. Maybe you'd best not say anything in the future to remind him."

After breakfast, Abby started her round of chores. On her way to the chicken coop, she paused on the outskirts of the small family graveyard. Instantly, something odd caught her attention. Abby gasped with a start! She dropped the bucket of feed, its contents scattering in the dirt. She began to scream.

Martha ran from the house in a panic, as her husband raced home from the fields. Abby continued to scream.

"My Lord!" Martha exclaimed. "We didn't intend for you to see that. We forgot all about it! It's been there so long."

Directly in the center of the graveyard stood a high stone cross towering over the other tombstones. Engraved upon it was Abby's name, the year of her birth, and the date of her captivity.

Wasting nary a second, Henry Colter paraded directly over to the cross. With a grunt, he laboriously lifted the tombstone from the ground. His face twisted in physical distress before sending the marker smashing to earth. Without a word, he returned to the fields.

Martha squeezed Abby's shoulders tightly.

"It was easier for Papa to believe you were dead. He'd endured so much grief already."

Abby pulled away from her mother. Solemnly she entered the small graveyard. Head bowed, she knelt between the graves of her two younger sisters, Lorrie and Ella.

"I remember back during the war, when the cholera claimed them, along with my best friend Mae Bishop. As if things weren't bad enough then."

"And you decorated all these graves with big batches of bluebonnets, your favorite flower," Martha said as she knelt down beside her.

Abby looked over at the tombstone just beyond.

"Mama, I miss Kynan. I could confide anything to him. He always understood."

"Your big brother would have been twenty-one years old were he alive. It was his savage and senseless murder at the hands of redskins that broke Henry inside. He's never been the same man. Your papa's always blamed himself for your capture. Years ago he failed to protect Kynan, and later you. That's an overbearing anguish in one man's mind and soul."

"But it wasn't his fault," Abby murmured. "It wasn't anybody's fault."

"No, but Kynan's absence will always weigh heavy upon us all." Martha sighed. "I often grieve for my tiny Lowell as well. A stillborn baby leaves a particular kind of emptiness in a woman's life."

Abby took a deep breath and tossed her head back. She almost seemed to swoon. Martha quickly rose.

"Are you all right?"

Abby took another deep breath and nodded. "I just felt dizzy and weak inside all of a sudden."

"After all you've been through, I'm not surprised."

That night Abby retired to bed directly after supper. She had done little work, but felt strangely exhausted. Although sleep was slow in coming, deep and troubling slumber eventually did.

That stone cross looming in the cemetery pervaded her dreams, accompanied by raging, voracious flames. Terrifying, exploding gunfire haunted her, along with gleaming sabers and their grisly mutilations.

Shrill screams of horror permeated the farmhouse and darkness. Abby sprang up in bed! Her alarming wails soon changed into the sounds of a wounded animal.

Henry Colter raced into the room with his Sharp's carbine at the ready. His bleary eyes darted wildly around. Abby could almost smell the fear in his sweat. Behind him stood Martha, a lantern held high and bright.

"Child, what's the matter?" her father demanded to know.

"They slaughtered them all!" she screamed through tears. "The women, the old folks, even the young 'uns! The cavalry butchered them in cold blood."

"You should be grateful they did," her father told her matter-of-factly. That was probably the only good those God damn miserable blue-bellies ever did their entire despicable lives."

"But so many were defenseless!" Abby protested. "And the soldiers murdered them! I feared they would kill me, too!" she cried.

"It's over. You're safe now," Mother reassured her.

For long endless nights to come Abby churned and twisted in her bed, entangling herself in her blanket. Vividly, she would relive the ruthless massacre. Her nightly terrors were a constant cause of woe, and upset her parents' sleep. Also her spells of dizzy weakness occurred more frequently, and were often more severe.

Her mother suggested a trip into town might be a pleasant change and do her some good. Reluctantly, Abby agreed.

Early the following morning, Abby and Martha Colter took the buckboard into Wildwillow. They reached town around noon. As soon as she stepped down from the wagon, Abby felt conspicuous.

"Folks are staring at me as if was stark-naked," she whispered.

"It's only your imagination," her mother whispered back.

Abby knew differently. Condescending, suspicious, cold stares greeted her wherever she walked. And her mother seemed to be invisible.

Abby forced a smile as she greeted familiar townsfolk along the way. Her greeting was returned with a nod or a tip of the hat, but not one with a smile or an inquiry as to her welfare. Some even glared at her with contempt.

On their way from the General Store, Abby noticed half-breed Navajo buck Jovah Two-Crows, the stable hand. He had always made her feel uneasy. Tensely, their eyes locked. In the past, when she caught the half-breed staring at her, he would look quickly away. Now it was Abby who turned away self-consciously.

As she and her mother were carrying supplies to the buckboard, Abby heard giggles and taunts of 'squaw woman' from the children. As she turned, the children quickly scattered.

Beyond, was a group of young ladies she had known since childhood. They whispered and snickered among themselves. The word 'whore' was repeated loudly. Abby glowered back and took a menacing step in their direction. Martha quickly seized her arm.

"Let it pass! It's the Christian thing to do."

As the two women were busily loading the buckboard for the journey home, someone grabbed the heavy sack of flour from behind and tossed it into the wagon.

Abby whirled around. "Chad!" she exclaimed in astonishment.

A tall ruddy-faced boy with light tan hair smiled upon her.

"Good to have you back. We were all praying for you." He beamed. "Let me buy you ladies a meal over at the café."

Abby politely refused, explaining they had eaten a basket of chicken and biscuits they'd brought from home, but she thanked him for the offer.

Martha Colter suggested that he stop by the farm sometime for a visit. Chad was noticeably delighted by the invitation. He grinned broadly as the two women waved and bid him a fond farewell.

"Even as little kids, Chad Hamilton always thought you were sweet as a berry tart," Martha reminded her daughter. "Today, he was right tickled to see you again."

"The rest of Wildwillow didn't seem to share his elation," Abby replied.

"I suppose most folks just feel awkward."

The following afternoon, as Abby stood unfastening laundry from the clothesline, she spied an approaching rider. The girl squinted, shielding her eyes from the blazing overhead sun.

"Chad." She swallowed deeply. Nervously, she began fussing with her hair, using her one free hand. A lace petticoat fell from her arm.

The boy pulled his horse to an abrupt halt and eagerly dismounted.

"Here, let me help you with that," he enthused. Quickly, he recovered the petticoat from the ground and began unfastening other items from the line while flashing his familiar grin.

Abby was overwhelmed and speechless.

"You know that Indian mustang you were riding? Some kids were throwing rocks and sticks at it. I led it out of town, and turned it loose. Now he's free, too, just as you are. Sorry I missed you that night."

Abby froze, her shoulders tensed. "Chad, the townsfolk in Wildwillow…I thought most of them were close as kin. But yesterday, I felt like an outsider. The way they stared." She shuddered. "I felt downright filthy."

"Some of the cavalry men said you were Chief Raging Storm's squaw," Chad did not look her in the eye as he spoke.

Humiliated, Abby dropped the laundry basket. She turned and fled into the farmhouse. Hastily, she brushed past her puzzled mother.

A few seconds later, Chad approached and asked to speak with Abby alone. Mrs. Colter eagerly obliged.

"Everything has changed," Abby lamented. "No matter how hard I try to pretend it hasn't, there's always someone to remind me. I've changed most of all. Oh Lord, everyone knows! How can you speak to me at all, Chad?"

"My feelings haven't changed," he told her sheepishly. "After your capture, I actually hated myself for never coming forward. Now I realize I have a precious second chance."

A lengthy silence hung between them.

"Let me fetch the laundry basket and you can help me fold," Abby said at last. "Maybe you'd like to stay for supper."

Before long, Chad Hamilton was spending nearly as much time at the Colter farm as he did at home. Frequently, he would present Abby with colorful batches of wildflowers. Often they strolled the fields behind the farmhouse. Sometimes they would picnic up in the hills, or enjoy long, leisurely rides on Chad's horse.

Martha laughed merrily to her husband. "I think we may have a wedding soon!"

"I sure wouldn't mind marrying up with Chad," Abby remarked. "He's more handsome than I remember."

"That Hamilton boy is one fine catch, with his papa being a well-to-do banker," Henry said.

"No one has money nowadays. Not like they used to before the war," Martha reminded him. "Land values have fallen drastically. Everyone's hurting. Still, if you marry Chad you can live in town. You won't end up as a farmwife. I'm not complaining, but it's a hard lot for a woman."

"I wouldn't mind it," Abby said dreamily.

"Why, that young man is like medicine." Martha clucked. "I see an amazing improvement. Those howling nightmares of yours haven't roused us from sleep in weeks. I do believe you're putting on weight too."

Abby retired to bed with a sensation of glowing bliss. Her peace of mind was at last returning. She slept contentedly into the wee hours of morning. Gradually, she became aware of hushed whispers emanating from the next room. She rose, and crept stealthily to the door to listen. Her parents were by the hearth, trying unsuccessfully to keep their voices down.

"Ester Hamilton glared at me that way, too!" Henry Colter was saying to his wife. "Why, she wasn't civil enough to return my greeting. And with her boy so sweet on Abby too."

"I just can't go back to sleep either," said her mother. "Might as well get the coffee started."

Shaken, Abby returned to her bed. She had no desire to hear anymore.

The following afternoon, she awaited the arrival of her suitor with uncertainty. Always in good spirits, Chad Hamilton cantered right up to the farmhouse on his two-year-old quarter horse. Abby was polite, but nervous. She remained quiet throughout the evening meal.

Afterward, she was anxious to get Chad alone outside.

“Let’s walk a distance from the house, away from any eavesdropping,” she whispered.

Chad’s eyes gleamed as he grinned, while Abby led him to the far side of the barn.

Abby glared him straight in the eye. “How come your folks have never invited me to visit?” she wanted to know.

Chad’s impish grin vanished. He paused to think, and measure his words. He took a lengthy breath before he spoke.

“They don’t want me getting serious about any girl. Not until I’m on my own.”

“Are you serious about me, Chad?”

“I want to marry you Abby, but I don’t know if it would be a good idea to live in Wildwillow.” He swallowed. “Folks here know about your past and they’re not a mind to forget.”

“My past?” Abby exclaimed in disbelief. “You’d think I was a two-bit slattern. Do they think I ran away with the Apaches? Or that Chief Raging Storm asked my permission before he made me one of his squaws?”

“Well, folks can be downright unreasonable, and cruel. I don’t want you being subjected to that the rest of our lives.”

“Guess it goes with the territory when you take up with a soiled woman.” She sniffed.

Chad grasped Abby’s slender hands and pulled them tightly against his chest.

“We can leave Wildwillow behind, and start our lives together far away.”

“No!” Abby replied with a huff. “We’re staying! We’ll stand together and confront everyone.”

The fierce tension on Chad’s face made him appear ill.

“Give me a little time to prepare my folks.” He gulped. “In the meantime, let’s keep this between you and me.”

After Chad departed, Abby was greeted by furtive glances and knowing smiles from her parents.

"Evening before last, you and that young man were smooching so hard, I could actually see sparks flying through the darkness," Papa said.

"Quit it!" Mrs. Colter implored. "Remember back when we courted? Why, you were the most brazen suitor of the lot! I slapped you down so many times, I'm amazed your face ain't permanently deformed."

"Oh, Abby doesn't mind my jesting."

"Child, you're mighty quiet."

"I was just thinking," she said. "My life is finally coming together at last. Everything is going to work out. I can feel it!"

Three days later Martha prepared a basket of food, as Henry rigged up the buckboard for a journey into town.

"May I come too?" Abby pleaded. "I'm tired of hiding out here. I'll make folks get used to seeing me again," she told them emphatically.

"You gals go ahead. I'll stay here and finish my chores," her father urged. "The trek will do Abby good."

Once in Wildwillow, Abby's bravado began to wane. Again she was greeted with disdainful, sour stares. And she could not help but hear loud whispers of "squaw woman."

Jovah Two-Crows was seated outside the livery stable. As soon as he noticed Abby, he rose to his full height and stared fixedly upon her. The scorn of the townspeople had made him bold. The half-breed had a way of narrowing his dark eyes that made his long, thin face appear weasel-like.

Abby shuddered. She looked around for Chad. The lad must have been running an out-of-town errand for his father. He was nowhere in sight. Martha and Abby quickly made their rounds, both eager to depart Wildwillow.

As they stepped outside the Dry Goods Store, Abby's head began to spin. She forced a couple of shaky steps toward the buckboard before collapsing in the dirt street. A curious crowd gathered and stepped suffocatingly close. Soon Dr. Nathaniel was summoned.

"Bring her to my office!" he ordered.

Sam, the hulking, brawny blacksmith darted from his shop and pushed his way through the tight crowd. He lifted the young girl in his arms as Abby began to regain consciousness.

She was given a thorough examination as Martha Colter waited and prayed nervously in the next room. Afterward, Abby felt assured she was well enough to return home. But Dr. Nathaniel and her mother insisted she remain for further tests.

The two women did not return to the farmhouse until well into the night. Henry Colter was standing outside waiting with his rifle.

"I feared maybe there were still savages about!" he told them with obvious relief.

Several days passed, and still the Colter's received no word from Dr. Nathaniel. Abby's father hitched up the buckboard in darkness long before the sun arose. He had already departed for town by the time Abby awoke.

"Henry had a few items to purchase at the General Store. He also plans to pay Dr. Nathaniel a visit," Martha told her daughter.

Abby's mother behaved unusually edgy and anxious. However, Abby herself appeared not a bit concerned with the doctor's diagnosis. In fact, she hummed contentedly to herself as she daydreamed throughout her chores.

The buckboard came clanking home an hour before sundown. Martha raced to greet her husband with Abby following closely behind.

Abby noticed her father appeared distressed. His face was more ashen than usual. He glanced nervously down at her, his expression between anguish and despair.

Martha took a deep apprehensive breath. "Henry, what did Dr. Nathaniel say?"

His body seemed to quiver and go limp before he spoke. "Abby's going to have a young 'un," he replied bluntly.

# Chapter Two

"What?" Abby exclaimed in disbelief.

"Oh no!" Martha wailed. "I feared it might be that. Please Abby, tell me the baby's Chad's."

Abby was too stunned to speak. Again the dizzy weakness spread though her. Her father jumped from the buckboard as Martha seized her firmly about the waist. Both helped her inside the farmhouse. They placed her into a chair.

"Is Chad the father?" her mother repeated.

"You know plum well he ain't!" snapped Abby.

"Well, you damn certain won't birth any bastard redskin in this house." Her father was adamant.

"We need to start looking for a way to get rid of it. Before it's too late. Before it sees light, I mean. Don't worry," Martha assured her.

Abby appeared incredulous. "What are you saying? This is your grandchild I'm carrying."

"No kin of mine is going to be a damnable heathen Apache." Henry bristled.

"But my child is half Colter. And Colters stand by our kinfolk. You've always said that Papa!"

"This is different Abby," her mother interjected.

"No it ain't! What you're saying is sinful. How can you even claim to be Christian folk?"

"We're not talking about a Christian child here," her father reminded. "We're talking about an Indian savage."

"A half-breed young 'un will lead a detestable, wretched life, and bring the lot of us grief," Martha added.

"God is testing our faith, as He did when the little ones died, and Kynan was murdered. Also when I was taken captive. We must stand firm," Abby stated.

"God not only understands, He condones it!" Henry snarled. "Scarred inside my brain forever is the memory of what those filthy, blood-lusty savages did to your brother. Never will I forget that day four and a half years ago when I came upon Kynan's body up in the hills. He'd been butchered and scalped." Henry almost gagged. "I'd sent him hunting. They probably murdered him for a doe. The act was so brutal and senseless." His eyes teared. "Indians are not human beings. They are mere animals bereft of soul. How can you even consider this?" her father implored.

"Can't you understand?" Abby beseeched. "This child is my blood. The same as Kynan. The same as yours."

"Colter blood shall never be contaminated. Not while I live!" Henry declared. "The Apache is a parasite among humanity. War and stealing is all they know, other than hunting. The Apache looks down on farming and chores that we do. You know that, Abby! Oh, and never forget, torture is considered sport. They sometimes even bring their young 'uns into the aftermaths of bloody battles and raids. The little ones torment and mutilate anyone still breathing."

"My child shall be civilized," Abby declared. "God-fearing Christian as we are."

"Be reasonable." Her mother sighed in exasperation.

"I am not the one being unreasonable!" Abby's voice rose in frustration. "I'm going to do what's right by my flesh and blood. My mind is set."

The following afternoon Chad showed up unexpectedly at the farm. The anxious lad jumped from his horse, and ran near-stumbling to Abby's side. His expression of anguish and distress mirrored her parents.

"We must make plans, I didn't know about the baby before."

"The baby! How did you know about any baby?"

"Wildwillow is a small place, Abby. Secrets don't keep well. Besides, most folks said it was obvious."

Abby closed her eyes tightly. Tears began to stream down her cheeks. "This changes everything," she whispered.

Chad pulled her against his chest. Gently he rested his chin atop her head. He softly massaged her back to reassure her. She pulled away.

"You don't want me as your wife anymore."

"Of course I do," he exclaimed. "But we definitely can't remain in Wildwillow. That's for certain."

"I suppose." She nodded sadly.

"We'll get married up in the northern territory," he continued. "After the baby's born, you can give it to a mission. Then, you and I can begin our life together. Maybe someplace in California. They say the Pacific Ocean is a magnificent sight to behold." His eyes gleamed with hope.

“My child is not an orphan.” Abby bristled. “Not while I’m alive. You want me to abandon my own blood!”

Chad was startled and perplexed by Abby’s reaction. “I’m thinking of what’s best for us all,” he explained.

“No! You’re thinking of what’s easiest, and not what is the right thing to do.”

“But why? Why would you even want this child after what you were forced to endure among the Apaches?”

“It’s my blood, Chad. I hoped you might understand.”

“What about Chief Raging Storm? Did you love him? Did you enjoy him touching you? Is that why?”

“No.” Abby winced.

“I don’t believe you! I should have listened to my folks. Everyone was right. The savages changed you! They soiled your character, as well as your body!” Abruptly he turned and hastened toward his horse.

“Then go!” she screamed through tears. “You’re the worst kind of bastard! Get off this property!”

Chad shook his head sadly. “I’m sorry Abby. But I don’t want any reminder of Chief Raging Storm around us.”

Abby watched him gallop away at full speed. She felt herself pale and sicken inside. Late that evening the horrible nightmares resumed in full graphic detail. Again, Abby’s piercing screams disrupted the entire household.

Early the following morning she discovered her father hitching up the buckboard.

“Your Mama’s taking you to see Dr. Nathaniel. It’s for your own good.”

Abby dreaded another sojourn into town. She cringed as the many rectangular buildings came into view. A small cluster of people were gathered near the physician’s residence, along with their horses and buggies. The Colters were forced to halt their buckboard down the street and walk.

Benton Foss, the tailor, cleared his throat and spit directly in front of Abby, nearly striking her. Others now turned and glared, watching her every move. The taunts of ‘Squaw Woman’ sounded louder and more accusatory this time.

“Someone’s got a little Raging Storm in her belly!” A man shouted. Others snickered.

"Keep your head high," Mother urged.

As Abby entered Dr. Nathaniel's residence, she was greeted by more frowning, disdainful, and curiously gawking faces in the waiting room.

Later, Dr. Nathaniel seemed to scowl as he spoke her name. She reached for her mother's hand. Together they quickly walked into the office.

The doctor cleared his throat and coughed before he spoke. "Abby, this is Chief Raging Storm's child is it not?"

Abby lowered her eyes, and nodded.

"So, what shall we do about it?" He sniffed.

"What do you mean?"

He peered at her over his wire-rim spectacles. "You have several options." He reached down inside a drawer. Instantly he placed a tiny, purple bottle atop his desk.

"This reads, DO NOT TAKE WHILE PREGNANT. It may produce the desired results. If not, I know of an old woman who lives on the outskirts of Jaxton Bluff. She can take care of it. The procedure is rather costly but…"

"No!" Abby bolted from her chair. Her body shook as she spoke. "What type of healer are you? You're not supposed to kill!"

"I'm only concerned with what's best for you," he said firmly. "Certainly you're upset, Abby. Now sit back down, and we'll explore this further."

"No!" Abby clenched her teeth. "We won't!" With that she stormed from the doctor's office into the foyer.

Martha Colter hurried after her. She grabbed her daughter by the shoulders. "Dr. Nathaniel is right, child. You're not thinking clearly."

Abruptly, Abby jerked away from her mother's grasp.

"You should be ashamed. You all should be ashamed!" Hastily she stepped outside.

Abby faced a large and more hostile gathering than before. The now familiar label of 'Squaw Woman' assailed her ears repeatedly.

"How could any decent Christian woman allow such a shameful thing to befall her?" shouted a female voice from deep in the crowd.

"You should have forced them to kill you at the massacre! Only a whore would come back here!" a man hollered.

The crowd began to jostle Abby. Someone shoved her. Martha screamed. Abby caught her balance. She began to fight back, pushing and shoving her way to the buckboard. A young woman grabbed Abby tightly by the hair. A man seized her arm, and began twisting it behind her.

With a loud painful grunt, the man quickly released her! Someone was now fighting right along beside her. Chad! Freed, Abby turned and struck the face of the girl who was yanking her hair. She then ground the heavy heel of her boot into the toe of a high-laced shoe as the young lady howled like a coyote in heat. An older, heavy-set woman lunged for Abby.

Earsplitting gun shots were fired repeatedly into the air! There were gasps, before the street fell silent.

"You have no right to judge!" Chad hollered. "Not one of you! Leave these fine ladies in peace. You people ain't Christians. You're barbarians!"

No one challenged Chad. Certainly not while his Smith and Wesson was drawn and smoking. By the time the deputy sheriff arrived, the street was nearly deserted.

"You really shamed 'em good." Mrs. Colter sighed.

"I won't forget this, Chad. I'm deeply obliged to you." Abby smiled,

"I'll escort you out of town," Chad offered.

"Why don't you come back to the farm with us, stay for supper?" Abby said invitingly.

Sadly, he shook his head. "I'm sorry," he muttered.

"I'm sorry too, Chad," Abby replied. "I'm grateful for what you did. But you don't need to escort us anywhere."

As evening arrived, a silence ensued between mother and daughter as they stood side-by-side washing and drying the remainder of the supper dishes.

"I wish I could send you to live with your Aunt Eudora in Sweetwater," Martha spoke at last. "Unfortunately she's too fragile. Eudie's still grieving over the death of your Uncle Daniel."

"But that was years ago."

"Poor little thing swears she'll grieve for that man the rest of her days."

"But eventually time will cure her grief," Henry remarked dryly, as he entered the kitchen.

"She's nearly ten years younger than I am. Not to mention a far sight more fetching," Martha added.

“You can’t stay here, Abby,” her father said bluntly. His face was as gray and furrowed as a death mask. “Not with that half-breed bastard in your belly.”

Abby should not have been surprised, though in fact, she was shaken and startled.

“We are not forsaking you, child. You’re our blood. You’re all we have, Abby.” Henry reached inside his jacket and produced a fistful of cash. “Here,” he said. “This is our family savings. Modest though it be, it’s better than nothing.”

Martha began to weep and fled from the room.

Fingers trembling, Abby took the money from her father. “I don’t know where I can go,” she murmured.

“Tomorrow I’m going to wire the Rev. Thomas Gregory and his wife Evangeline. They were close friends to your mama once. I’ll purchase a ticket to Clatterwood over in the New Mexico territory,” Papa told her. “They’re decent folk. They won’t turn you away.”

Mrs. Colter beckoned to Abby from the next room. Before her was a small, wooden jewel box. “These belonged to your grandmother.” Inside were a pearl ring, a cameo pin, a triple-strand necklace, and a cameo choker. “I had planned to present them to you upon your wedding day. Take them with you.”

“I’m never going to return am I, Mama? My life here has ended."

# Chapter Three

The afternoon was a swelteringly bright and arid one as the stage pulled into Clatterwood in the New Mexico territory.

The town displayed stark rows of rectangular wooden buildings uncomfortably similar to those back in Wildwillow.

Abby stepped down into the dirt street. She glanced around tensely as the coach was being unloaded. When she reached down for her valise, a tall man with sandy hair suddenly appeared before her. He wore an ecclesiastical collar.

The woman who stood beside him was trim and sturdy-looking, with a plain but pleasant face. Both appeared to be in their early thirties. The couple introduced themselves as the Gregorys.

"Mercy!" exclaimed Evangeline. "You have Martha's striking blue eyes."

"Let's get this lovely young lady away from the dusty street. Here, I'll take your bag," the Reverend offered.

The Gregorys resided in a small house behind a stark-white church, located in the far corner of town. The living quarters were minimal. Abby's room was compact and sparse, with one high, tiny window and an extremely narrow single bed.

Abby dabbed the sweat from her face and neck before putting on a fresh calico dress. Afterward she joined the Gregorys in their modest parlor.

"When's the little one due?" the Reverend asked as he placed a bookmark in his bible.

Embarrassed, Abby felt herself redden. She had a strong desire to turn around and run back into her room. "In the Fall." she murmured. Her voice was almost a whisper.

"You need not be ashamed," Evangeline responded as she rose from her chair. "It wasn't any fault of yours."

"In fact I admire your strength and fortitude," the Reverend added. "Your ordeal would have broken many others."

Mrs. Gregory placed a comforting arm about Abby's shoulders. She squeezed the young girl firmly against her chest. "We'll give you both the best care we can offer."

"I don't want pampering," Abby declared. "I'm a diligent work hand. I intend to earn everything I receive."

"What type of chores do you prefer?" inquired the Reverend.

"Not that I'm choosy, but I'd rather labor outside. I feel a greater energy outdoors."

"Just like my Evangeline!" He smiled broadly.

"Why, I can't abide being caged indoors during the prime of the day." Mrs. Gregory rolled her eyes. "And I still miss climbing those tall, fragrant pine trees back in South Carolina."

"Oh, back in Texas I did most of the hunting after Kynan was killed," Abby told them. "Sometimes I'd pause for a swim in a stream, or mountain lake. Often, I'd climb a tree and wait for game. I had a clear view of everything below. And I'm a crack shot!"

"Actually, the only indoor chore I really enjoy is baking," Evangeline said. "I can bake a greater variety of breads than a big city bakery, not to mention an assortment of fancy pastries of every description."

"At age twelve I could out-bake my mother," Abby said with pride. "My sweet potato pies were famous in Wildwillow."

"Come help me prepare supper and we can chat," Mrs. Gregory said as she reached for Abby's hand. "Already I prefer your company to all these boring heifers and dreary scarecrows here in Clatterwood."

Evangeline and Abby shared much in common. Their friendship deepened as they quickly and eagerly confided in each other. Mrs. Gregory soon became as close as kin to her young charge.

Before long, Abby's belly began to swell. Both women had to busily re-tailor Abby's clothes to fit her new fuller contour.

"That child's going to be a boy," Evangeline told her matter-of-factly.

"And how do you know that?" asked an incredulous Abby.

"Easy," Mrs. Gregory replied. "You're carrying the baby high under your breasts. That's a boy! A girl child is carried low in your belly."

Abby still appeared incredulous.

"Just wait. You'll see." Evangeline nodded.

Later in the evening Mrs. Gregory was urged by her husband to pay a social call upon a parishioner who was feeling poorly.

The Rev. Gregory helped Abby clear the supper dishes as the reluctant Evangeline departed. She bid them good-bye with a grimace.

"I'm surprised she chose this life," Abby remarked.

"She didn't choose it," he informed her. "I did, and she chose me.

I sometimes wonder if she regrets it."

"Evangeline is the most contented and happiest woman I've ever known," Abby assured him. "In spite of her complaints."

"And you are the most courageous. I admire you so fiercely. Most would have taken the easy route."

"I was tempted, Reverend," Abby admitted with a sigh.

"But you didn't! You have the strength of your convictions. Do you know how rare that is?"

"Well, the Almighty came through for me. He delivered me from the Apaches. How could I ever let Him down after that?"

"You are well suited to this life indeed. Abby, you are a godsend."

Embarrassed by his praise, Abby lowered her eyes and smiled sheepishly. As she reached down for another plate, their fingers awkwardly touched. The Reverend quickly seized her hand before she could withdraw.

Startled, she stared directly into the deep, gray-blue of his eyes. To her surprise, he was trembling. The Reverend slowly drew her slender fingers up to his heaving lips.

Abruptly, Abby jerked her hand away. "I need no help," she snapped. "Go sit down. Supper's over."

The Reverend stiffened self-consciously. His face was flushed and sweaty. Silently, he backed away.

The following morning at breakfast Evangeline complained non-stop about her mercy visit with the sickly parishioner, Gloriana Peary.

"That old gal is what you call a hypochondriac! The only thing sick about her is her mind. The skinny buzzard has the entire congregation agitated with her theatrical deathbed act. And I could see she had you mighty worried, Thomas. Last night when I returned, you were in your bedclothes kneeling and praying in the chapel with an intensity I have never before seen."

The Reverend Gregory paled. Nervously, he excused himself from the table.

"You're mighty silent this morning," Mrs. Gregory said to Abby.

"Oh, I'm just listening and thinking." Abby began to feel guilty. Perhaps she had misunderstood the Reverend, and caused him needless chagrin.

Thomas was sympathetic and completely non-judgmental. He was a good man. Certainly she was genuinely fond of him, as she was Evangeline.

The next time their eyes met, she greeted him with a warm, generous smile. He at first blushed, but eagerly returned her sentiment.

Over the next few days Abby began to study the Reverend closely. His strong, clean features had always reminded her of Kynan. Yet he was as different from her late brother as he was similar. Before long, Abby was seeking out his council on a frequent basis.

As her body continued to swell, Abby's pain increased. The Reverend became fawningly solicitous of her, far more so than his wife, Evangeline.

"Stop mollycoddling her, Thomas!" Mrs. Gregory would holler. "She's just carrying a baby. She's not one herself!" Also the softness had disappeared from her voice whenever she addressed Abby.

Feeling confined, and growing uncomfortable around Evangeline, Abby ventured into the heart of town alone. The time was late afternoon. As she stepped down into the dirt street to cross, Abby recoiled in disbelief.

Over to her left, less than a block away stood Jovah Two-Crows, Wildwillow's Navajo half-breed. Eyes narrowed he stepped forward toward her. The half-breed had a way of moving that made him appear like a stalking cougar about to pounce.

Heart pounding, Abby stepped back. She turned and fled in a panic. She raced all the way back to the church. As she tried to catch her breath, Abby collapsed before the Reverend and his wife.

As she regained consciousness, Abby discovered Evangeline gently wiping her face and neck with a cool, soothing cloth.

"The baby's coming. It's going to be fine," she was told.

"Is it true that Navajos are a branch of the Apache tribe, and they speak the same language?" Abby inquired with insistence.

"I don't know," Evangeline answered with a hint of irritation in her voice. "Rest now. Take it easy until I tell you what to do."

Mrs. Gregory's theory had proved correct. At 1:24 the following morning Abby gave birth to a baby boy. The child was named Blaine, after her mother's side of the family. The Reverend Gregory and his wife Evangeline presented the new infant with a small, white-bound bible inscribed to Blaine Colter.

"He is the fruit of God. Teach him well," the Reverend said to Abby.

Motherhood soon enveloped Abby's life. Before long, Blaine was one year old. Evangeline grew all the more distant. The Reverend eagerly took on the role of father to Abby's son.

Early one evening Mrs. Gregory attired herself in her hat and shawl. She scowled at her reflection in the narrow hall mirror, likewise at her husband and Abby as they played happily with Blaine.

"I realize you won't miss me. I'm attending a quilting bee at the Peary house. Of course, I loathe that sort of activity. But at least those catty bitches don't make me feel non-existent." She huffed as she hastily departed.

"Evangeline has grown to hate me," Abby lamented.

"I've always wanted a child. My wife is barren. You're an ever-present reminder." He sighed wistfully. "It wouldn't even have to be my own flesh and blood...God help me! I wish you were my wife, Abby."

"I wish it could be, too," Abby confessed at last. She reached for his hand and firmly squeezed it.

The Reverend pulled her over across his lap. He seized her waist. Instantly Abby's lips met his, for one long desperately clinging kiss.

Blaine began wailing loudly beside them. Soon passion had succumbed to shame, regret and guilt; unbearable guilt. The Reverend hastily retreated to his chapel. After attending to her child, Abby stepped outside to allow the refreshing coolness of night to sweep over her.

Through the darkness, she spied something moving stealthily towards her. Abby squinted for a closer look. The shadowy outline of a man gradually took form. Jovah Two-Crows!

Abby fought the urge to scream. She stepped back inside, bolted the door, and tried to calm herself. She began scribbling a note to the Gregorys.

Hours later, Abby, with her infant son, waited at the stage depot. The early morning sun had risen anew. Soon a coach would carry them far away, into a distant territory.

# Chapter Four

Abby and her small son arrived in the Colorado territory during the midst of a magnificent Indian summer. The high altitudes were breathtaking. Aspen trees nearly everywhere and oaks, maples and birch trees were vividly attired in reds, yellows, russets and browns. Soft glades, abundant forests and vast meadows were everywhere.

The town of Durango was surrounded by dense Aspen forests, their leaves a strikingly beautiful shimmering gold and copper. Durango's streets were wide and bustling. The numerous houses all seemed to possess spacious, open porches. Toting her valise in one hand and her son upon her hip, Abby checked into a rundown boarding house.

The following morning she applied for a position as cook at a large hotel. She was informed they wanted an older woman. She applied at several dress shops as a salesgirl. Later, she went to a bakery. At each place she was rebuffed. Every position required a woman with experience. Abby could not even get hired as a servant.

Eventually, as the days and weeks passed, Abby was forced to pawn her grandmother's heirlooms just to pay the rent. Leaves quickly dropped from the trees followed by the freezing cold as snow fell. Abby went hungry to feed Blaine. But soon there was no money remaining for food or rent.

Chilled to her marrow, Abby had no heavy clothing suited for a Colorado winter. Swallowing her pride, she marched into a Mercantile Store. In near tears, Abby begged for work, any work.

"Come back in spring," the owner said. "We might have an opening then."

"I can't wait that long!" Abby exclaimed. "I have a young 'un to feed and tend. We'll perish before spring. Please!"

The portly little man appeared sympathetic. He reached inside his pocket and handed her a few silver coins. "I'm sorry," he said. "This is all I can do."

Abby sniffed, and took the coins. She turned toward the door. Half way there, she fell to her knees and began to sob.

Tears streamed down her face, blinding her, as her body rocked and shook. Abby heard whispers around her. To her surprise, she suddenly felt a woman's arms surrounding her, comforting her.

Someone wiped away her blinding tears. Beside her was a small, middle-aged woman with a wiry frame. Her delicate-boned face was narrow, with a firm jaw. "Nothing can be that terrible," the woman intoned.

"Who are you?" Abby asked in astonishment.

"I was born Sadie Dooley. Now where do you live? I'll take you home."

Abby introduced herself, before explaining her desperate situation. It was the last day she could afford a room at the boarding house.

"Come with me," Sadie said. "I've work aplenty for you. And a roof over your head, too."

Sadie Dooley accompanied Abby to the boarding house to gather up her meager possessions. As they entered the lobby of the old building, they were greeted by the shrill sound of Blaine's bawling from upstairs.

"Can't you keep your little bastard quiet!" hollered an elderly patron. "It's been a'wailing for hours like a fornicating cat!"

Abby glared at her coldly as she raced up the steps followed by Sadie. The young mother swept Blaine up into her arms to quiet and reassure him. Sadie stared at them both with mouth agape in astonishment.

"Yes, he's half Indian!" Abby declared. "Apache in fact. I suppose you don't want to hire me now." She snuggled Blaine beneath her chin.

"It's not my place to pass judgment on anyone." Sadie took the baby from his mother's arms, freeing Abby to gather her modest belongings.

"What sort of work will I be performing?" Abby wanted to know.

"I'm an overworked seamstress. You'll be my assistant. Here, take your son. I'll carry your valise."

Abby, with child in tow followed Sadie on a long walk clear across town. All of a sudden, she was startled to discover they were standing directly in the center of the infamous Tenderloin district.

"What are we doing here?" she asked in puzzlement.

"We're employed right over there." Sadie pointed to a huge, ornate structure with a spacious veranda extended over its vast open porch. A handful of painted and colorfully attired women peered curiously at them from both levels.

"That's a bawdy house!" Abby exclaimed. "How could you think I'd ever work in such a vile place?"

"I suppose you and your milksop would rather starve!" Sadie sneered.

Abby shivered in the frosty cold as she tightened her grasp on her son. "I'll sew clothes and that's all."

"That's all we agreed upon," Sadie confirmed.

Again, Abby swallowed her pride as she carried Blaine inside the notorious Honey Belle Saloon. The young farm girl was awed by what she found.

The vast interior was nothing short of palatial, with its broad swirling staircase and numerous gigantic crystal chandeliers. Satin couches and brocade velvet curtains were decorated mostly in red and gold. On the walls was an extensive gallery of nude artistry that almost caused Abby to swoon from embarrassment. For a moment she wondered if it was all a bizarre dream.

Through an adjoining door Abby spotted an elaborate stage overlooking a long horseshoe-shaped bar. From that room a swaggering, heavy-set woman emerged. Her hair was a startling white although her round face appeared youthful and unlined.

"I see you brought me a new young filly!" she enthused.

"This is my new assistant seamstress," Sadie informer her.

The woman looked at her in disbelief, and then at Abby.

"I'm Honey Laycock. And that's my true name too. Well, the Laycock part anyway. Sweetie, when you're ready for a real job, come and talk to me."

"No, thank you!" Abby snapped.

"Come, our quarters are in the back," Sadie led the way. "A word of advice, don't antagonize Madam Laycock. She pays both our salaries. Your room is over there."

"Why it's lovely!" Abby exclaimed in astonishment.

"Wait until you see the ones upstairs. They are absolutely grand. Honey just hired six new girls and they require costumes. The rest of them also need another set. Plus their garments get ripped a lot." She winked.

Abby was kept constantly busy. However, she was able to keep one eye on Blaine as she worked. Madam Laycock continued to pester her about taking an upstairs job.

"You'll haul in some mighty impressive cash. Many of my wealthy gentlemen have noticed you. They were damn disappointed to learn you weren't on the bill o' fare. Don't you want to wear costly brocaded silk and velvet, and precious jewelry, and French parfum? Hey, with your assets you'd be able to retire in luxury, long before you ever lost your figure. Think about it!"

"None of those things would mean anything if I lost my self-respect," Abby told her.

"If I didn't know you had a papoose in the back room, I'd swear you was a virgin. You talk as foolish as one." The white-haired woman snorted.

Abby had written letters to both her parents and the Gregorys to inform them of her well-being. After several months she received a reply from the Gregorys only.

She was stunned and hurt by what she read. The once non-judgmental Rev. Gregory informed her God would severely punish even a seamstress in such a shameful establishment.

Abby wrote back that God already punished her and she had done nothing wrong.

Certainly her parents must have been distressed and ashamed by her news. Thus the silence. Perhaps she should have disclosed nothing.

Sullenly, Abby joined Sadie and busied herself adding final embellishments to the evening's costumes. They were interrupted by Madam Laycock.

"We're ready!" the Madam hollered.

Sadie tossed the garment down beside her. "My services are required upstairs." She sighed wearily. "Heat up one of the darning needles in the hearth. Then bring it up to the Lilac suite."

Puzzled, Abby did as instructed.

Inside the Lilac room was Jollie, a girl Abby's age. She was heavily bundled in wool comforters. The room was icy. Jollie's cinnamon-colored tresses hung in long curls over the bed. Her expressive hazel eyes appeared tense and frightened.

Another whore named Ophelia sat by her side with a bottle of whiskey. She was half dressed and shivering.

"You may leave now," Sadie told her. She ordered Abby to take her place. "Hold up her head, and keep her good and drunk."

Perplexed, Abby picked up the bottle and noticed it half empty. Jollie already had a head start.

Sadie lifted the thick covers at the foot of the bed. Abby saw the glint of the darning needle.

"What are you doing?"

“Don’t pay no mind to what I’m doing. Just do your job.”

Jollie cried out! Abby gasped. The bottle dropped from her grasp. It smashed into pieces on the floor.

“Clean up that mess right now!” Sadie hollered.

Appalled by what she had just witnessed, Abby stood frozen in horrified disbelief. Sadie had to physically shake her to make her hear.

“You took out her baby!” Abby screamed into Sadie’s face. “You killed it!” She turned to confront the drunken Jollie. “How could you let her? Your own young’un. Your own flesh and blood!” she shrieked.

“I’m a whore’s daughter!” Jollie shrieked back. “You think I want a young’un to end up like me?”

Disgusted, Abby fled the room. She raced down the long, swirling, marble staircase to her quarters. Sobbing, she quickly began to pack her possessions.

Abby picked up Blaine, and reached for her valise to leave. Sadie grabbed the handle at the same instant. Abby was startled to find her standing there.

“Now where are you going? Put that down.”

“I’m going as far away from here as I can get. Let me go!”

“Very well, but leave the boy here. If you want to starve, then go! But leave the child where he has food and a roof over his head.”

“You hypocrite! You don’t care about him. I just saw you murder a baby!”

Sadie rolled her eyes in exasperation. “I did it a merciful favor. It was for the best.”

“Only God should take a life. You’re not God.”

“No, but I sent its little soul to be with Him along with many others. He should be obliged to me for doing His work, and saving Him the trouble.”

Blaine let out an ear-splitting howl.

“Life is not sacred, never was. It’s the most expendable commodity ever created,” Sadie continued.

“You’re as barbaric as the Apaches!” Abby exclaimed in disgust.

“Life is cruel. Perhaps we’re just being practical.”

“I won’t hear this heathen prattle. God will deal with you upon the Day of Judgment. There’ll be an agonizing eternity of hellfire as payment for your deeds!”

Blaine cried out loudly again. Abby tightened her grasp upon the boy.

"You sure remind me of my pious parents and their stinking self-righteous friends back in Illinois." Sadie jerked back her long, wool sleeves revealing ugly scars.

Blaine continued to bawl with abandon. Abby stood in silence.

"There are scars in here, too!" Sadie said, as she firmly clutched her chest. "Some people should never be allowed children."

"I'll pray for you," Abby murmured.

"Do it, but don't you dare judge me! You are not God either. Go ahead and leave if you must. Starve and freeze for your convictions. Get out of here!"

Blaine wailed so loudly customers in the lobby could now be heard complaining. Abby retrieved her valise. She turned to leave, looked out the window at the blowing, freezing snow, cringed and shivered.

She hesitated at the door. Slowly, she turned, and dropped the valise. She pulled the still-bawling Blaine closer to her breast.

In the coming days the guilt and despair almost seemed to overwhelm her. Abby was sullen and spoke little.

"Snap out of it!" Honey told her. "Your glum demeanor is depressing everyone in this weather. I need major alterations on three costumes. The girls will be down any second. Now smile!"

The three were Opal, Bess and Divinity. Abby set to work. The trio griped constantly. They forced Abby to make needless alterations and then snickered at her frustration.

"Guess sodbusters are too stupid to do anything except pull a plow," Opal drawled.

"It's all that intermarrying down in Texas," Divinity explained. "Heard some of them even breed with farm animals, while others breed with red-skinned savages."

Seething, Abby jabbed Divinity in the thigh with her sewing needle. The woman screamed, then shouted out an obscenity. She kicked the kneeling Abby onto the floor.

Abby quickly jumped to her feet. She lunged at Divinity. Both women tumbled onto the carpet; punching, kicking, scratching and pulling each other's hair. Frightened, Blaine began crying in the corner.

"Keep your Injun bastard quiet!" Someone hollered from the next room.

Abby was sitting atop Divinity, pummeling her with tight fists, when Sadie and Madam Laycock arrived to pull them apart.

"She jumped me!" The battered whore pointed toward Abby. It's her fault!" Opal and Bess backed her up.

"You're discharged," Madam Laycock told Abby. "You and your brat are nothing but trouble. Now clear out!"

"Wait," Sadie interjected. "She's a fine seamstress, and I need the help. At least let her stay until I can find a qualified replacement."

Reluctantly, Madam Laycock relented.

"That one can be blind when it comes to her girls," Sadie told Abby later.

"Those whores stare at me as if they'd like to kill me," Abby muttered.

"And how do you stare at them? Like they're scum on the bottom of a chamberpot, that's how! No wonder they're antagonistic towards you."

The following afternoon a letter arrived for Abby. The return address was Wildwillow. However, it was from Aunt Eudora. Curious, Abby tore it open quickly.

The words at first seemed too unbelievable to register. Staggered by the news, Abby was too numb to cry.

"My folks are dead," she related to Sadie in a shaky voice. "Mama died suddenly of a stroke. Same afternoon Papa put a shotgun in his mouth and pulled the trigger." As she spoke the words out loud, the tears began to flow unbridled.

Later that evening, after she had rocked Blaine to sleep, Abby quietly left her room. She could hear a bevy of Laycock girls performing on stage. They were stomping and squealing out a ribald song, while men whooped loudly in delight.

Abby sneaked up the back stairs. From behind the balcony she was able to observe the show unnoticed. She was startled by the unnatural appearance of the performers. They looked like pretty, painted puppets. Though it was the midst of winter, the women danced near-naked in their scant gaudy costumes. She felt a combination of pity and contempt for them.

The enormous room was jammed with noisy customers. The wealthiest and most influential men in Durango must all have been seated in the plush balcony just beyond. Many were merrily tossing gold coins down onto the stage as they hollered boisterously to gain a performer's attention.

Abby imagined their prim families waiting in their lavish, comfortable homes. She recalled her own folks, and growing up back in Texas. All their lives had been such an arduous struggle filled with so many senseless hardships. The Colters were God-fearing, decent, honorable people and diligent workers. Yet they died so far in debt, every cherished possession had to be sold.

Abby wondered why God only rewarded the undeserving. There had to be justice in heaven, because surely there was none on earth.

Months passed and spring arrived in Durango. The dense Aspen forests were again lush with foliage. Conifers were now decorated with yellow clusters, while the fresh blue of spruce trees was restored.

As the new season blossomed, Sadie's upstairs services were frequently required. The first was Jessica, a former aristocratic Georgia belle who lost everything, including her self-respect, in Sherman's march to the sea.

"Are you going to help, or are you going to fall apart and throw a tizzy-fit again?" Sadie inquired as she confronted Abby. "I won't force you." She sighed in resignation. "Let me see if one of the fillies is available."

"I'll assist you," Abby murmured.

"What did you say?"

"I'm your assistant. I'll help you. I'll try to ease her pain, and nothing more."

Several weeks later, Opal required Sadie's service. The next was Neysa, an Alabama sharecropper's daughter left orphaned and destitute by the war. She was followed by Imogene who lost her husband and family to the same cause. Others, like Regina, refused to discuss their past.

"I want you to pay careful attention, and watch closely," Sadie instructed Abby. "I'm getting arthritis; someday you'll have to replace me."

"Never, never while I live," Abby vowed.

"Sure you will. Just you wait." Sadie chortled.

Soon, a year passed, and then another. Abby thought constantly of leaving the notorious Tenderloin district for a more respectable job. She had no desire to see Blaine grow to manhood in a saloon. However the pay was steady and their quarters were more than adequate.

By the third year, Abby seemed resigned to her position there, at least for the time being, until she could save up enough money for a small farm.

The Colorado sun was harsh in mid-summer. The hills and meadows were aflame with red wood lilies and fireweed. Everyone seemed particularly short-tempered from the heat.

Abby was sent beyond the Tenderloin district over to the Dry Goods Store to purchase several bolts of taffeta for Sadie.

Upon her return trip, she became aware of voices directly behind her. Two men were following uncomfortably near. They whispered to each other. Abby overheard filthy lewd remarks concerning her appearance.

"Yeah, that's her, that prissy one from the saloon."

Abby was about to run. Suddenly she was seized from behind! A rough hand was clamped tightly over her mouth. She struggled and fought while the other man grabbed her feet. She felt herself lifted through the air.

"We're not only gonn'a get it, we're gonn'a get it for free!" The one behind her chuckled.

Abby writhed and twisted as she was carried between the buildings into a cluttered alley. She was thrown onto the dirt. The large, sweaty hand again clutched her face so tightly, she was almost suffocated. The men began grabbing her and tearing at her clothes.

Strangely, one of the men was screaming! The other one now shrieked and released her! Abby saw the flash of a Bowie knife. Its blade was stained and dripping scarlet.

As the two men fled, Jovah Two-Crows appeared out of nowhere. He stood directly over Abby, gazing down upon her.

# Chapter Five

Slashed and bleeding, the two men fled for their lives. Jovah had adroitly disarmed them of their guns. Abby stared at the half-breed in apprehension and disbelief as she lay in the dirt. Suspiciously, she watched him.

Jovah slipped his Bowie knife back into his moccasin boot. Squinting, he stepped forward and extended a hand to her.

Still shaken and suspicious, she backed away. "Don't touch me!" she shrieked. Abby quickly scurried to her feet. "Get away, you hear me!" she screamed.

The half-breed stood expressionless as she abruptly brushed past in a panic. The long bolts of taffeta were left behind in the dirt street. Sadie later retrieved them.

For several weeks, an anxiety-ridden Abby remained cloistered inside the saloon. Annoyed, Sadie deliberately sent her upon another errand to the Dry Goods Store, threatening to discharge her if she refused.

"Every time you been thrown and stomped by an ornery mule you've got to get right back on top and seize those reins again," Sadie told her, as she began sending Abby on more and more errands outside the tenderloin district.

Weeks passed. Upon her way to the bakery, Abby stopped in her tracks. She spied Jovah Two-Crows laboring outside a livery stable.

For a brief moment, he gazed at her. But soon his eyes were downcast, the way they used to be, before her capture. He proceeded grooming a horse.

Abby swallowed hard, unsure of what to do. Acting more out of curiosity then courage, she walked slowly towards him.

"Why have you been trailing me?" she demanded to know.

Jovah stared at her with an expression of dismay. He flung the horse brush down into the pail with a loud clunk. Abby stood firm.

"It doesn't matter," he mumbled, as he lowered his eyes again. He clicked his tongue, and began leading the horse inside.

"I want to know!" Abby shouted after him.

Jovah turned. He narrowed his eyes. "I couldn't abide the way you were treated in Wildwillow. Everyone turned on you, even your folks. I thought you would need someone to look out for you."

Abby felt her mouth drop. Still, she was suspicious.

"Hey, I'm not a savage!" he hollered. "I was educated by Jesuits. I can read and write. And well, too!"

She watched as he led the horse inside to a waiting stall before she continued on her way.

Barely another week had passed before Abby encountered the half-breed again. Jovah was standing outside the General Store. He was engaged in conversation with another man, a tall stoop-shouldered but muscular fellow with dirty-blonde hair.

The man turned. He had a flat nose and thick lower lip. Something about his demeanor caused Abby to feel uneasy.

To her relief, the other man departed. She stood face-to-face with Jovah.

"Thanks for coming to my aid that time." She tried to force a smile, but was unsuccessful. "You shouldn't have come here because of me."

"You were just an excuse. I was eager to leave. At least the faces have changed." He shrugged.

"Exactly how long have you been here, in Durango?"

"Almost a year and a half now." Jovah sniffed. "Spent most of that time working on the Donovan ranch, until the opening at the livery stable last spring."

"You mean Willet Donovan? He comes into the Honey Belle on occasion."

Jovah nodded. "I've seen you in town a few times before you saw me. But I kept out of sight. Didn't want to spook you again. Thought I'd lost your tracks for good the last time."

"Actually, I had other reasons for leaving Clatterwood," Abby confessed.

The two continued to chat as they walked. Soon Abby and Jovah found themselves inside the Tenderloin District.

"I can't believe you're living here." He shook his head. "A lady like you, among these lewd, painted women. It seems a sacrilege somehow. Like putting a diamond on the same necklace with a string of cheap rhinestones." His voice displayed genuine sadness.

"My son and I must survive." Abby sighed. "We have nothing else."

"That's not true. You have a friend to depend on, close by. Remember."

"That's a comforting thought. Don't hide yourself from me anymore, Jovah."

Abigail Colter and Jovah Two-Crows more and more began seeking solace in each other's company. Often they received disapproving stares from passers-by. But neither cared. Everyone else had become insignificant.

Abby's life at the Honey Belle now seemed less of a trial. She was actually becoming friendlier with the Laycock girls, as well as pleasant to the regular customers; men like the rowdy Hogan Reeves, the boastful Sam Hooper, the parsimonious Ethan Tuttle, and the laconic loner Pete Black. The time now passed quickly. Yet every second she longed for Jovah's company.

"Watch your moves with him," Sadie warned. "I've seen that half-breed drunk with Slick Larsen, one of the most unsavory men I've ever come across. If you ever shake hands with that vermin you'll not only feel dirty, you better count your fingers as well."

As frigid, winter cold returned to the territory, Abby took seriously ill. The doctor's diagnosis was pneumonia. Jovah was devastated.

"My younger brother died from pneumonia, and our father did nothing," he lamented.

Jovah rode thirty miles non-stop through the raging snow to an Arapaho reservation. There, he purchased rare medicine herbs at his own expense.

During his absence, Abby's condition worsened. The doctor had given up hope of recovery. Jovah took temporary residence in the cellar of the Honey Belle. He ground some of the herbs into powder and boiled others. He prepared Abby's meals and remained by her side.

His position at the livery stable was lost, but Abby was not. Her convalescence was quickened by his presence and the healing Indian herbs.

Madam Laycock immediately forced Jovah from the saloon.

"I don't want to be accused of selling spirits to a redskin! He's been seen coming and leaving. I could go to jail!"

"You don't have to worry," Abby assured her.

"Oh yeah? I sure smelled whiskey on his breath. And you have too!"

Abby was unable to deny the truth any longer. She realized the half-breed must be confronted, for both their sakes. In the early evening darkness, she hurried over to the old, ramshackle boarding house in the Tenderloin district.

As she stepped nearer to Jovah, she inhaled a pungent whiff of alcohol.

"You shouldn't drink so heavily!" she snapped.

"We were celebrating," Jovah exulted. "Slick got me rehired, back at the livery stable."

"The Madam doesn't want you around the saloon any more. You stole liquor from the Honey Belle, didn't you?"

"How ungrateful can you be!" he shrieked into her face. "You'd be a frozen slab of meat by now if not for me!"

Abby turned to leave.

"It was the only way I could cope!" he cried out. "I was so afraid you would die. I couldn't bear such a thought. I would have killed myself had you died, Abby."

Ashamed, Abby hastened to Jovah with arms outstretched to comfort him.

The following spring was a frigid, icy one. And the soothing warmth of summer seemed late in coming.

"Thanks for watching Blaine," Abby hollered to a reluctant Sadie, as she hurried out the door. Abby rushed excitedly to meet Jovah for a picnic. They rendezvoused on the rugged outskirts of Durango.

"I've never seen a land so magnificent or as grand as the Colorado Territory," Abby remarked. "However," she added, I long for the gentler Texas winters."

"The glorious beauty here is worth the harsh cold and misery of a seemingly endless wait," he replied. "Sometimes we must endure the horrendous, infernal torments of purgatory. How else could we truly appreciate paradise?"

"Back in Wildwillow, I never imagined we'd be together this way, Jovah, talking and laughing as we do. Back then, it seemed unthinkable." She lowered her gaze.

"The first time I saw you, it was your shimmering hair I noticed. The way it's sun-streaked, the color of ripe maize. But always, I've admired the way you carry yourself. Head high, back straight, that proud walk! I could bask in the glow of your presence."

"You speak poetic words. You amaze and mystify me, Jovah. You're so clever at times."

The half-breed appeared suddenly affronted and indignant. "Why is that remarkable? Because I'm an Indian? The Jesuits educated me well. I used to read the classics and I wrote poetry. I longed to continue my education, but I lacked money." He shrugged sadly.

"Jovah, I wasn't trying to put you down. Honest! I was complimenting you."

"You can't imagine what it's like. You just can't imagine."

"Let it pass, Jovah. We're both beginning our lives anew together. The ugly past is dead." She threw her arms tightly about his waist. "I love you."

His sullen expression faded. His tawny face now beamed elation. Awkwardly, his arms began to encircle Abby. She tightened her grasp.

"I must be daydreaming again," he whispered.

"There's one way to find out for certain." She smiled invitingly.

They clutched tightly again, and kissed deeply. Slowly, the entangled couple dropped to their knees in the high grass.

Abby returned to the Honey Belle as dusk began to fall. She glided from room to room. Blaine raced to greet his mother. Briskly, she swept the child up into her arms and hugged him affectionately. Sadie's lips twitched as she watched.

"Jovah and I are going to be married," Abby enthused.

"Oh, I hope it's not for the reason I suspect." Sadie's eyes narrowed. "Have you gone too far?"

"No. But we came awful close."

"You need to think about this a lot more."

"Why? Because Jovah is half Indian? Well, so is my son. Blaine is five years old. He needs a father."

"I see moonbeams dancing in those blue eyes and that's a feeble reason to wed. Remember, it's far easier to get trapped into marriage than to escape from one."

"It's God's will that Jovah and I be together. And I had actually begun to doubt. Well, the Almighty has come through for me again. Jovah is my guardian angel."

Sadie threw up her arms in exasperation. "Don't go blaming God for your damn fool folly a few years down the path. Marry your mistakes and you're forced to live with them."

"I'm going to remain here for a while. Jovah will continue at the livery stable until we can save up enough money for a homestead. We're looking forward to becoming a family. Blaine will have an excellent father.

The following afternoon Abby hurried to meet her fiancé in front of the livery. The half-breed stood amicably talking with that same light-haired flat-nosed character she had seen before.

As she stared, the man turned to face her. He licked his thick, lower lip salaciously, as he ogled Abby obscenely. It made her flesh prickle.

“See you later,” he said to Jovah.

“Who is that?” Abby wanted to know.

“Slick Larsen. I’m going to ask him to be best man at our wedding.”

“Never! You didn’t see that lewd expression when he looked me over. I felt like one of Honey’s girls.”

“Slick likes to tease the ladies. Don’t take offense. It wasn’t personal.” Jovah shrugged.

“I’ve a sick feeling about that man. Keep him away!”

“Abby, he’s the truest friend I’ve ever known. He’s become as close as a brother.”

“I don’t want him around, Jovah.” Abby was adamant.

The half-breed lowered his eyes in resignation. “So when do we fetch a minister?”

“Sadie is making me a dress. When it’s finished. Madame Laycock wants us to marry in the saloon. Guess she’s forgiven you. Judge Hoopersmith is a regular at the Honey Belle.”

The gleaming, white gown adorned with layers of fine, intricate hand-made lace, felt scratchy and binding to Abby.

“I made it for sheer beauty, rather than comfort,” Sadie told her.

“The judge is waiting!” Honey screeched out from the main parlor.

The Laycock girls all gathered reverently about the couple. Their attire was so conservative, Abby had difficulty distinguishing them at first.

Soon she and Jovah Two-Crows were pronounced man and wife. Honey Laycock had agreed to let them honeymoon upstairs in the governor’s suite for the night.

“Wait! Before you start enjoying yourselves, we have a little nuptial gift for you,” Honey said. She produced a paper the judge had drawn up and handed it to the bride.

Abby excitedly read the deed. “We have a farm!” she exclaimed. Abby stooped down to hug Blaine. The lad stood quietly by her side with a beaming smile.

"Now, don't expect it to be much. It's just a modest place to get you started." The Madam's eyes moistened. "I dismissed you once. It's long past time you left."

Abby fondly embraced Honey and each of the Laycock girls in turn. Her warmest farewell was reserved for Sadie.

The Two-Crows' family homestead turned out to be a small miner's shack with a tiny shed out back. The place was surrounded by high rocky hills.

"Honey said not to expect much," Abby said to a scowling Jovah.

"That's our home!" Blaine excitedly shouted. He quickly jumped from the back of the buckboard and raced to explore.

"I'm going to begin planting a garden over there." Abby pointed to the left of the shed. "We have enough money saved to buy a cow, and some chickens, too. This place will be a farm, Jovah. Just be patient."

"I'm beginning to miss town already," he replied with a sniff.

Abby and Jovah began unloading. They headed toward the old miner's shack. The boy flung open the door to the tiny back shed and entered.

"Look! There's a crate of firecrackers in here!" he exclaimed.

"Blaine! Put that back!" Abby hollered in alarm. "That's dynamite!" Blaine was scolded and told never to touch them again.

The following day a visitor came to call. Abby recognized him as Ethan Tuttle, a Honey Belle regular.

"We're neighbors," he told the family. "I almost purchased this property once."

"Are you still interested?" Jovah asked sarcastically.

"Nope, don't need any more land."

Abby made coffee. She invited Mr. Tuttle to remain for the noonday meal. He whipped out a large, unusually ornate antique gold watch and gazed at the time.

"Thanks anyway, but I don't want to disappoint my cook," he said. "Some other time perhaps."

Jovah curiously watched him ride away. "Wonder how much we could actually get for this place? A farm might not be right for us."

Abby turned sharply in surprise. "We have land to plant roots, that's important to a family, Jovah."

Her husband remained silent.

Months passed, and soon another frigid Colorado winter returned. Jovah was creative at finding excuses to leave. He spent more and more time in Durango while his family remained home. His sojourns grew lengthy. Often he would return during the wee morning hours.

"I fret for you," Abby told him impatiently. "Riding home alone in darkness through that blinding snow and ice is downright perilous."

"I come from strong stock." He bristled. "I'm Indian. Indians are not frail, like whites."

"You're only half Indian, Jovah. Besides, your place is here with you kin."

"I'd go stark raving crazy if you forced me to stay! I feel like a wild creature confined to a small cage. How can you tolerate this place?"

"I suppose because I'm too occupied with my chores, and yours! I'm too exhausted to even think most of the time." She sighed.

"Abby, why don't we sell this miserable land? We could travel up to Denver if you like?"

"No! Before we married, you and I longed for a farm and to settle down. Remember?"

"You wanted a farm. I never did! If not for that meddling old whore we'd never have been stuck with this wretched place!"

Blaine began screaming from his bed. Abby rushed to his side in the adjoining room.

"There was a fiery shot and blood everywhere, Mama! Until I opened my eyes." He bawled.

"Our fussing woke him up," she said to her husband. "Blaine loves this farm. It's his first true home. We're a complete family, Jovah. I intend to keep us together no matter what it takes."

By summer, Abby found herself toiling alone beneath the hazy, sweltering Colorado sun. Her tanned complexion was nearly as brown as Jovah's. The planting was long finished. She knew that in August she would be harvesting the wheat herself. Blaine was of some help, but still too young for any major labor.

The fence-mending completed, she would now take the old Hawken rifle and go hunting up in the foothills. In the evenings she tutored her small son by the light of a lantern.

Jovah returned late one morning. He was singing loudly as he led an extra horse behind him. "I won this fine animal from Sam Hooper, betting on a cockfight."

"You lose plenty more than you win," Abby reminded him. "You waste what little profit we have on your gaming. And you stink! You're reeking of liquor."

Jovah curtly brushed past her.

Abby produced a bottle of whiskey. "I found this hidden in the shed out back. Where did you get it?" she demanded. "You're half Navajo. No one is allowed to sell you liquor."

Jovah glowered at her contemptuously. "Slick purchased it for me. Best friend I've ever known. My blood brother."

"Well, no more! Either stay home or clear out for good!"

"A woman does not tell a man what to do. Never!" Jovah seized the bottle from Abby's hands.

She charged forward. "Give me that!" She struggled with the drunken half-breed. The bottle, three-quarters full was flung forcefully against the wall. It shattered into thousands of gleaming fragments.

Eyes blazing hellfire, Jovah glared at her like a coiled diamondback ready to strike. Enraged, he drew his fist and struck her savagely in the jaw. As Abby attempted to rise from the floor, Jovah kicked her brutally in the stomach.

Blaine came running from outside. "Mama! Mama!"

Indifferently, Jovah stepped over her semi-conscious body as Abby writhed in pain. Through blurry eyes she watched as he staggered toward the bedroom to sleep the day away.

# Chapter Six

Abby was doubled over and vomiting blood outside the tiny porch, when Jovah awoke hours later. Blaine sat by her side trying to comfort her.

"It's your fault! You did this! You're bad!" The boy screamed wildly at Jovah.

The half-breed appeared dazed. He stared down at Abby in disbelief. "Oh God, no," he muttered. Tears welled in his dark eyes. He walked over to Abby and dropped to his knees.

"You're the only human being I've ever honestly loved. And I could have killed you. God punish me, I've become like my father!" Jovah pleaded Abby's forgiveness.

The ugly experience genuinely seemed to have a profound and sobering effect upon him. Jovah remained home, and became solicitous of his wife and Blaine. As Abby recovered, he labored at every chore, without complaint, no matter how menial or arduous.

Jovah took the buckboard into Durango for supplies. Upon his return, he presented Abby with a gift wrapped in streaming blue ribbons.

She was astounded to discover a ruffled, low-cut, satin ball gown as deep blue as her eyes. "Wherever am I going to wear this?" she asked.

"You'll wear it for me. We'll exist in our own world, our paradise. The way we once did."

"Jovah, we own a farm, not a gold mine. Return it. We desperately need the money."

"But I thought you'd be pleased."

Abby took a deep breath. "I'm touched by the gesture. But I declare, Jovah, sometimes I don't think you have the common sense God gave a goose."

Seething, Jovah slammed his fist down on the table so hard the entire farm seemed to quake. "Damn you," he sputtered. "I can't do anything to please you! Nothing makes you happy. You're impossible!"

Furiously, he departed, slamming the door behind him. Abby heard the pounding hoof beats of his horse as he rode away. The following morning, he returned home drunk.

Several weeks passed, and one day, as Abby toiled in the field, a strange rider approached. A letter was personally delivered, the return address Wildwillow. Aunt Eudora was currently employed as housekeeper to Dr. Nathaniel.

Abby was heartbroken to read that Chad Hamilton had wed a pretty red-haired lass from Alabama. The two had recently departed for San Francisco.

Abby shoved the letter deep inside her apron pocket and continued her labor. She was determined not to cry.

Later, alone seated upon her bed before candlelight, she read the dreaded words again. Before long, she found herself weeping bitterly into her apron.

Without warning, the bedroom door flew open. A drunken Jovah staggered inside.

"I thought I wouldn't see your face before dawn." She sniffed as she wiped away her tears.

"You going to give me more grief? Oh, what's the matter? You been bawling like a brat. Hey! What's that in your hand?"

Abby quickly tried to stuff the letter back inside her apron pocket. Jovah lunged at her. He grabbed at the apron. Before Abby could stop him, he was bending over the candle reading her correspondence.

"Jovah, give that to me," she demanded.

Swiftly he swung around. "I'll give you this." He struck her hard across the mouth with the back of his hand. "You weren't good enough for Chad Hamilton! The banker's son didn't want your little bastard half-breed, did he?"

Abby tried to fight Jovah off, but he seized her by the shoulders.

"Don't you ever get uppity with me!" he screamed. Jovah flung her forcefully to the floor. "No one else but a half-breed would have you after the Apaches."

As Abby tried to climb to her feet, Jovah grabbed her by her hair. She clawed at his face with her nails until his skin was bloody. He brutally began slamming her head against the wall.

Abby heard a scream. Blaine was standing in the doorway.

"Stop! Stop!" he shrieked. The boy threw himself on his stepfather's back. Blaine pounded on him with tiny, clenched hands.

Jovah sharply whirled around, throwing the boy to the floor. He kicked Blaine before pummeling him with tight fists.

"No!" Abby screamed as she scurried between them. She wrapped herself about Blaine to shield him from Jovah's heavy blows.

Exhausted, Jovah finally relented. He paused for breath. "I'll finish you someday. I'll finish you both!" As he took another deep breath, he passed out.

Blaine buried his head deep in his mother's chest as she sighed with relief.

Jovah continued to spend most of his waking time in Durango. The farm chores fell behind while she throbbed in pain for weeks. Slowly, Abby recovered.

Early one morning, Abby hitched the buckboard for a journey into town.

Her hung-over husband emerged groggy and disheveled from the house.

"Jovah, shouldn't you be fast asleep?"

"Where you sneaking off?"

"Perhaps Sadie will do me a favor and buy this fancy dress. We sorely need the money. Blaine and I won't be home until late."

"That was a gift!" Jovah charged toward her. "It's not for sale." He jerked the garment from her fingers. "You never tried it on, never once." Teeth gnashing, Jovah angrily ripped the material to shreds before her eyes. "Get down," he ordered.

Blaine raced from the farmhouse carrying a basket of food.

"Go back inside. You're not going any place!" Jovah hollered. With that, he pulled Abby from the buckboard and shoved her into the dirt.

Abby hastened to her feet and fought back. Jovah grappled her from behind. The two struggled.

"This wretched farm was a gift, too. Yet you wouldn't sell it. Just my gift! You don't have any right to look down on me, not you!" Jovah flung her to the ground and kicked her.

Abby groaned in pain as he dragged her through the dirt and up the hard wooden steps of the shack. Shrieking, Blaine hurried to her aid. He was savagely kicked back by Jovah.

Two-Crows dragged his wife inside, and bolted the door behind them. As Abby screamed from his brutal blows, she noticed Blaine's teary face against the window, peering helplessly inside. Suddenly she felt sadder for him than herself.

Another year and a half passed. Abby and her son barely subsisted on the farm. The little money they had, she was forced to hide from Jovah. If not for her hunting skill with the old Hawken rifle, both might have starved.

To her distress, Abby began feeling dizzy and sick to her stomach. At first, she thought it due to Jovah's occasional beatings. However, as her belly began to swell, the reality became apparent.

Jovah berated her for becoming fat and slovenly.

"This extra weight is only temporary. By summer, I'll be slim again," she told him, half dreading his reaction.

A heavy silence elapsed. Jovah exploded with exuberance. "A baby? We're actually going to have a little one. I'll be a father!"

"We already have a fine son. The next young'un will only be a hardship."

"Don't say that! Our child could never be any such thing."

"Our resources are limited. There's much work ahead, Jovah. Blaine and I won't be up to it alone."

"This child will be part of us. Nothing is more important. I'll do whatever needs to be done," Jovah vowed.

Abby was skeptical. However, Jovah was true to his promise. To her astonishment, once again, he became the tender and sympathetic man she had first known. His heavy drinking and gaming were part of the past. Even Blaine began to respond to him again.

"This is exactly the way I wanted everything to be." Abby sighed contentedly. I've long been praying to God for a miracle. I just hope it lasts. She stroked her belly softly with the palm of her hand. A girl, she thought.

Mid-spring Abby gave birth to a daughter. Sadie Dooley had arrived from town to deliver the baby, accompanied by Honey Laycock.

"My word," exclaimed the Madam. "Look at those blue eyes. And with that fair complexion you'd never suppose she possessed a drop of Indian blood."

"Well, she does have Jovah's narrow face and high cheekbones, also his thick, jet-colored hair," Abby remarked. "I've never seen a small creature look so delicate, or perfect, so beautiful."

Blaine abruptly left the room as Jovah quietly entered. The child was christened Lorella Mae Two-Crows, after Abby's two young sisters,

Lorrie and Ella, and her best friend Mae Bishop, all of whom had perished from cholera during childhood.

In spite of her joy, Abby found herself deeply saddened after Sadie and Madam Laycock returned to Durango.

The arduous farm labor was beginning to exact its toll on Jovah. Frequently exhausted, he became short tempered and critical.

"For all these long, endless days of toil, there are little sustenance and less money," he constantly complained. "Farming is a fool's life."

Early one dusk, Jovah gathered together their meager savings. Abby caught him by surprise.

"What are you doing?" she asked with alarm.

"We need more money, and I intend to get it for us." He hurried out the door to his waiting horse.

"No! Jovah! Jovah, come back! Jovah!" she screamed as he rapidly rode away.

Unable to sleep, Abby paced the floor for hours. Jovah returned shortly after midnight with his shirt stuffed full of cash in small bills.

"I quit while I was ahead," he announced proudly.

"I don't like gaming money," she told him. "It's dirty. You didn't drink, did you, Jovah?"

"No, I would never do that again."

However, as he stepped past, Abby could not avoid smelling the stench of liquor.

The following week, Jovah again ignored his wife's protests and made another nocturnal excursion into Durango. Within the month, she was back to hiding money from him for the family's survival.

Jovah was heavily into gaming and drinking again. His violent outbursts had returned. He was easily irritated and impossible to pacify.

A drunken Jovah returned early one evening. The half-breed had been cheated in a cockfight and was in a particularly ugly mood.

Blaine accidentally bumped against him. Enraged, he flung the boy hard against the wall. Blaine fell to the floor half conscious.

Abby hurried across the room to help her son. Jovah intercepted her.

"Leave him be," he said. "Blaine is unworthy of his blood. He must learn to be a man."

"Oh? A weak, lazy drunk," she replied. Abby waited stoically for the ensuing blows, but did not regret her words; even as the pummeling became unbearable.

Lorella's earsplitting, shrill wails began saturating the small farmhouse.

"Shut that brat up!" Jovan shrieked. "Stop it, now! I can't bear her noise anymore!" He pulled his knife from the moccasin boot. His eyes blazed with malevolence as he charged toward the screaming infant.

The thunderous crack of a rifle boomed and resounded throughout the modest farmhouse. Eyes wide and glazed cold with surprise, Jovah Two-Crows fell dead upon the wood floor.

# CHAPTER SEVEN

Rifle in hand, Abby stood frozen in disbelief and denial. The atmosphere felt unreal, like a horrendous dream. She was oblivious even to the shrieking of her children. It was Blaine's persistent tugging on her skirt that brought the reality into focus.

"Jovah's dead! Jovah's dead!" he shrieked.

Trembling herself, Abby tried to calm him. "We must think of our own survival now," she told him. "No one must ever find out."

"There's a cave way up in the hills. We can hide him there," the boy said.

"You mean that old miner's shaft, son. I'll need your help. We can't wait until daylight."

Abby and Blaine constructed a horse-travois.

"Help me hoist the body. Now get me several sticks of dynamite from the shed," she ordered.

Abby mounted the horse. "I don't know when I'll return. It's so dark." She shivered. "I'll need a lantern."

Blaine insisted on accompanying her. However his mother was adamant that he remain and tend to his sister.

Through the darkness Abby trekked the steep, rocky slopes on horseback. Eventually she located the old, abandoned miner's shaft.

She unhitched the travois from the mare, then strung the lantern from the rope and hung it about her neck. Next, Abby firmly grabbed both sides of the travois and pulled Jovah inside the shaft.

Masses of loose dirt and gravel rained down upon her. The old shaft was supported by rotting wood. Abby feared she would be buried alive, to rest forever with Jovah.

Weary and frightened, she dropped the travois. She stood deep in the interior. Abby tore the lantern from her neck and drew the dynamite sticks from her apron pocket.

She knelt briefly by her husband's side. Softly, she stroked his face and hair. "Jovah, Jovah," she murmured. "Your trouble and my grief was that you possessed an excellent mind but a weak character." With that, she forced open his mouth and shoved the dynamite sticks deep in his throat. With one hand clutching the lantern, she lit the fuses and fled for her life.

Perspiring and heaving for breath, she emerged into the cold darkness of the night. She jumped on the mare and ground her heels mercilessly into its sides. Racing blindly through the darkness, Abby whipped the horse furiously every lap of the way.

In a split second the pitch darkness erupted and thundered behind her, exploding with such force that both the woman and horse were propelled down the mountain slope like sawdust dolls.

The wind knocked out of her, Abby wobbled to her feet. To her relief, the mare was also unharmed. But the lantern was shattered.

The following morning as Lorella slept, Abby and Blaine busily cleaned up the remnants from the night before.

"Someone's coming!" Blaine hollered with alarm.

"Abby hurried to the window. "It's Tuttle. Stay inside!" Nervously, she stepped from the shack to greet her neighbor.

Ethan Tuttle tipped his hat as he quickly drew near on horseback.

"Howdy, Mrs. Say, did you hear that big explosion in the night?"

Abby felt her stomach turn inside out. "No, uh no. We heard nothing."

"By golly it caused an avalanche! You certain you didn't hear anything? What about the children?"

Abby shrugged and shook her head.

"Is your man Jovah sleeping one off again?"

"Keep your voice down. He'll be in a foul mood if he's awakened." She forced a weak smile.

"Lord knows he didn't hear anything. But I'm surprised at the rest of you."

"I'd like to chat, Mr. Tuttle, but you caught me at a mite inconvenient time. I'm dreadful busy this morning."

The neighbor smiled politely. "Ma'am," he said, amicably nodded, and rode away.

Abby sighed with relief. Several days later, she and the children took the buckboard into town. The family stopped at the Honey Belle Saloon.

"I'm putting my property up for sale," she announced. "Jovah ran off and left me. The farm is too much for me and the young'uns."

Everyone appeared stunned, except Sadie.

"You won't get much for it," Madam Laycock said. "Forgive my bluntness, but it's hardly the choicest property in the territory. But at least it got you away from here."

"I'll take whatever it will bring. Spread the word."

Sadie accompanied Abby and the children out to the buckboard.

"You're awful eager to give up. Perhaps Jovah will return."

The expression on Abby's face told her otherwise.

"I might have guessed." The seamstress swallowed deeply. "A few months back Neysa saw you leaving the Dry Goods Store. She said one eye was so badly bruised, it was nearly swollen shut. I made that gal swear to silence. And I tried to get out to see you, but work tied me down."

Abby lowered her gaze in shame. "You warned me."

"Sell that land, scat the territory, fast! Get as far from here as possible."

"But I don't want to run again. I have a family."

"Listen, you don't have a choice, gal!"

Long months passed. Winter had come and gone. Still, there remained no serious buyers for the Two-Crow's land. In frustration, Abby hitched up the buckboard and paid a visit to Ethan Tuttle.

"You claimed once that you almost purchased my property, Mr. Tuttle. Please," Abby beseeched, "I'll consider any offer you care to make."

Tuttle fingered his antique-gold watch in the palm of his hand as he pondered. "I'll let you know," he said.

A week later he handed Abby an envelope full of cash in exchange for the deed. The amount was meager, less than half the original asking price. However, Abby was elated.

Almost immediately, she and Blaine loaded the buckboard with their belongings. Early the following morning, the family headed north.

Several hundred miles out of Durango, they spotted Comanche warriors. A raiding party emerged from a clearing in the forest below, within shouting distance.

Abby seized a startled Lorella and covered her mouth. She instructed Blaine to quickly hide the buckboard.

"Mama, I've never seen you this scared," Blaine murmured. "If they return, they will find us for certain." He urged her on. "We must keep moving."

"Well, I'm changing the route then. They came from the northeast, so we'll veer west!"

After another hundred miles of rugged terrain and wilderness, music began to permeate the air.

"Are we near a town?" Blaine asked.

“We shouldn’t be, not way out here.” Abby steered the buckboard to follow the sound of the melody.

To the family’s amazement, they came upon an enormous, populated valley. Hundreds of people were congested among dirty huts, tents and ramshackle buildings. Snaking through the valley was a shallow river filled with prospectors.

“What is this place called?” Abby hollered out.

“Welcome to Muddycreek!” Two drunken men answered in unison.

“Pleased to see you, Ma’am.” A short, stocky fellow pushed his way between them.

“I desperately need supplies. Is there a place here to buy anything?” she asked.

Abby was directed toward a poorly constructed wood frame building. The interior had a stale odor and was badly maintained. However, the supplies were plentiful.

“These prices are outrageous!” Abby exclaimed. “I’d go bankrupt if I shopped here.”

“These are the going rates in Muddycreek, Ma’am,” the clerk told her. “You can easily find employment in the valley. Why, I heard that Pastor Cooper’s camp is looking for a woman to cook and sew. They’d pay you well.”

Having no choice, Abby went in search of the Pastor, Cyrus Cooper. She sent Blaine back to the wagon with Lorella.

“Cooper’s tent is that one, over yonder.” The barber pointed.

The tent flap was tightly closed.

“Pastor? Pastor Cooper?” Abby called out. She heard commotion inside followed by a shrill laugh.

A woman emerged, attired only in a flowered choker and loosened corset. Giggling merrily, she waved a pair of red long-johns in the air as she darted past Abby and into another tent.

A tall man quickly emerged from inside. He stood buck naked. Abby felt her face flush. Irritated, the man made eye contact with the shocked Abby, before hastily covering himself with the tent flap.

“Pastor Cooper?” she asked in disbelief.

“Yeah. Who the hell are you?” he shouted.

“My name is Abigail Tw…Crowe. I’m a widow. I was told you need someone for cooking and sewing.”

Cyrus looked her over in detail and nodded with pleasure.

"I have two young'uns, an eight year old boy and an infant. Does that make a difference?"

"No, I'm plum grateful for a woman willing to work. Let me clothe myself and we'll clear our things out. You and the young'uns will need the tent."

Abby thanked him and went for the buckboard.

After she returned with her family, Abby learned there were three more men in the Cooper camp: Brady Campbell, Tuck McCreedy, and Jordy Spritler. The latter was the short, stocky man she had first encountered. The displaced prospectors began improvising a flimsy, makeshift hut for themselves.

In the neighboring tent, only a few feet away, dwelt two large men. The younger was muscular and handsome. The other was heavy with a coarse face. They appeared to be foreigners, both spoke broken English.

"That's Alexei Orlova and Pyotr Zverev. They come from a place called Rostov-on-the-Don. They're a couple, if you know what I mean." Cyrus winked.

"Uh, no. I don't," Abby said.

"I mean I married them, woman!"

Abby gasped. "That's blasphemy! What do the other men think of that?"

"Nothing, now." Cyrus shrugged. "At first a group of fellows organized themselves. They planned to run the Ruskies out of Muddycreek. However," he chuckled, "Alexei and Pyotr beat the pickled gut out of them."

"They're not a very domestic couple," Brady Campbell added. "Perhaps you can pick up some extra sewing there."

"Come on down to the creek," Cyrus beckoned. "As you can see we pan for the yellow iron, or what the Apaches call pesh-klitso."

Abby cringed nervously. Cyrus could not help but notice.

"Those two young'uns, they Apache?"

"My son is…I was captive." Abby raised her head high. She tossed back her hair. "The Apaches have come to value gold. Now they call it orohay."

"It shines just as pretty by any name." Cyrus gave her a sieve.

Jordy Spritler had cut a spruce sapling. He handed it to Abby.

"Stake out a section of the stream," Cyrus instructed, "but be careful. Twelve claim jumpers were shot to death just this week alone."

Awkwardly, Abby waded into the water in her long skirt. She had difficulty finding an unoccupied spot. Blaine came running from the camp. He helped her find one.

"Now slash the gravel and pan it," Cyrus continued. "If you're lucky, you'll find a scattering of gold nuggets. The real wealth comes from the mother lode. No one has located it yet. It's the mama vein that throws off the nuggets."

Soon Blaine was panning for gold right alongside his mother, and often alone, as Abby labored with her chores and tended Lorella. However, between them, they eked out little from the stream. The others in the camp seemed to fare better.

Frequently, a Conestoga filled with whores traveled to Muddycreek from Denver. These were not attractive women as in the Honey Belle Saloon. Most were plain with too much paint, feathers and ruffles. Often they were more ridiculous-looking than alluring.

One looked familiar. She was bony with a long neck and thin, pointed nose. Cyrus introduced her as Mariposa Jones. Suddenly, Abby remembered her as the woman who ran giggling from Pastor Cooper's tent. She had returned.

"I do Cyrus free," she announced bluntly. "With all the others it's just business."

Abby was speechless. Jordy Spritler led her away.

Later, as the women mounted the Conestoga back to Denver, Mariposa remained. Cyrus insisted she share the tent with the widow Crowe and family.

Abby could hardly refuse, since the tent belonged to Cooper.

"She won't spend much time there," Cyrus assured the young mother. "Remember, she's a working lady."

After years at the Honey Belle, Abby was more tolerant of whores. She tried to make Mariposa comfortable.

"Mostly, I'll just use this place to store my possessions," Mariposa said dryly. She was true to her word.

Several weeks had now passed. The hour was dawn. Abby emerged from the tent to begin breakfast. Cyrus stood stretching before his hut. Most of the others were sleeping one off. Every night seemed a festival at Muddycreek.

In the distance, Abby noticed a rider enter the valley. He appeared disturbingly familiar. Slick Larsen! Instinctively, Abby darted back inside the tent. She hushed her children as she peeked through the slit in the flap. She was certain he had not seen her.

Larsen rode over to Pastor Cooper. Courteously, he tipped his broad-brimmed hat. "I'm looking for a pretty, yellow-haired gal with two half-breed young'uns in tow. I believe she was headed this way."

Cyrus' face twisted as he pondered. "Hmm, I'd remember that…uh, wait a sec. Yeah, someone like that passed through here several months back. Believe they headed up toward Wyoming territory."

Slick hesitated a moment, then tipped his hat before riding away.

Abby waited a few seconds. In a whisper, she called out to Cyrus and beckoned him inside. She thanked him profusely.

"I pride myself on being a dandy judge of character. I'm able to see through people," the Pastor said. "Better wait in here awhile longer."

Cyrus departed, only to return several moments later, "You need a peacemaker." He placed a Colt 45 by her side.

"I have a Hawken rifle."

"But a six-shooter is easier to conceal. Keep it."

Brady Campbell prepared breakfast that morning, and Jordy took it to the family. Shaken, Abby completed her other chores inside the tent with her children. The Pastor was adamant. Later, McCreedy and Spritler scouted the surrounding hills for any remnant of Slick Larsen.

Abby was growing nearly as impatient as her children to leave the tent. The day dragged slowly by.

As darkness fell, Abby tutored Blaine by the light of a lantern. Lorella slept beside them. Mariposa entered to change into fresh clothes.

Abby ordered Blaine not to look around, only to concentrate upon his lesson. She made him name every single United States president right up to the present one. Afterward they discussed the role of vice president.

"Mama," Blaine asked, "if both the president and vice president were assassinated, who would run the country?"

Abby thought for a moment. "Why, I…I don't actually know," she confessed.

"The Speaker of the House of Representatives," Mariposa told them. "That's an easy one."

"And how do you know?" Blaine asked with suspicion.

"Because I'm smart, that's how."

"No, you ain't! You're only a dumb whore."

"Blaine, apologize!" Abby demanded. The boy ignored her and ran outside. Lorella was awakened by the commotion. Embarrassed, Abby apologized for her son.

"Whoring is just my part-time occupation," Mariposa explained. "The rest of the time I'm a prim and respectable lady back in New Hampshire. I was wife to the Mayor of a small town. Now I'm a widow just like you. I create and peddle floral scented soaps. In fact, the Mariposa Lily is my top seller. My husband left behind a stack of debts. Some men just can't handle finance. Mariposa Jones isn't my actual name. Not even Cyrus knows who I really am."

Abby was astounded.

"And would you believe half the whores in the territory are schoolmarms," Mariposa continued. They make twenty dollars a month teaching school. You can make that amount on a slow night here. And I know two other proper widows back home who do likewise. I'm surprised you haven't jumped aboard the golden wagon yourself, a comely woman like you."

"I couldn't, I'm a Christian."

"Well, I live for this world and damned if I'll be shortchanged. Life feels more natural here, more exhilarating. And then there's Cyrus."

Abby was puzzled. "What exactly is it about Pastor Cooper that interests you? Not that he ain't a fine man," she was quick to add.

"Cyrus is a fascinating contradiction. He's both the wisest man and the biggest fool I've ever known. As a practicing man of God in a small Tennessee hollow, he was run out and banished for his carousing and wicked ways. Heard he even raped a woman. But I think she asked for it. Yet he maintains a profound spiritual side that I can't reach." Mariposa shrugged wistfully. A deep sadness filled her eyes.

Abby walked over and placed an arm around her shoulders.

"My true name is Florence Montgomery," Mariposa volunteered. "Don't tell anyone, please." There was a note of finality in her voice.

The two women warmly embraced.

The following morning when Abby awoke, she discovered Mariposa had vanished along with all of her possessions. Blaine claimed to have heard her clearing out during the night. Alexei Orlova had also disappeared. His companion was devastated.

"Some folks just ain't faithful to their marriage vows," Tuck McCreedy drawled.

"I saw Mariposa putting rouge on Alexei's cheeks and lips, two nights ago. Then she wrapped a feather boa around his shoulders and kissed him," Jordy Spritler spoke up.

"Poor Pytor is already so besotted he'll be sleeping in vomit tonight," Brady Campbell remarked.

Abby comforted Pastor Cooper. "Mariposa deeply loved you. I don't understand it."

"I do," Cyrus said. "We thought much alike, Mariposa and me. But we were also different. We didn't really mesh. Mariposa was a Yankee gal, after all."

Before long, the weather began cooling dramatically. Abby was busy preparing supper as Pastor Cooper was doctoring Jordy Spritler's arm, swollen from a snake bite. Resounding shots of gunfire suddenly filled the autumn air.

"What's going on?" Jordy sputtered.

Cyrus dashed to his hut for a firearm. Abby rose from her kettle and glanced curiously about. She reached for Lorella and called out to Blaine.

Sounds of cursing along with gunfire were now heard throughout the valley. Campbell and McCreedy, equally vituperative, approached their comrades.

"Damn him! Miserable god damn bastard!"

"Hope he dies."

"Who? What's going on here?" Cyrus inquired.

"Someone hit the mother lode down the stream. A Swiss fellow named Franz Kohler," Brady explained. "We may as well pack it up. The dream is done for."

"It's dead," Tuck McCreedy added sadly.

"It ain't dead!" Cyrus bristled. "There are plenty of Muddycreeks in this vast territory. We'll just up and go find another."

The other men cursed under their breath. They seemed far less optimistic. Cyrus turned to Abby.

"Will you come along, please? We're all a family now."

Abby shook her head. "Your dream is not mine. Looks like we need to make it to Denver before the snow falls." She drew her children close to her side. Soon they departed the valley.

Denver was the biggest and most bustling city Abby could ever imagine. Lining the wide boulevards were numerous rows of red brick buildings, decorated with courtyards among intricate arches and stained glass domes. The mountains beyond formed a backdrop of extraordinary, majestic beauty. The children were awed to silence.

Abby had earned enough at Muddycreek for a modest, decent apartment. Almost immediately she whipped off letters to Aunt Eudora and Sadie Dooley.

Abby found employment as one of three subordinate cook/dishwashers to a chef at an upscale Denver hotel. The other two women were surly and snide, the chef arrogant and demanding. All of them condescendingly referred to Abby as 'that farm girl'.

To her regret, Abby was forced to leave Blaine and Lorella alone for long periods. Worry and guilt plagued her constantly. Often her concentration was not upon her chores. For this, she was hotly rebuked and ridiculed.

Before long, the family received a welcome letter from Ft. Morgan, north-east of Denver. Abby was surprised to learn that long-widowed Aunt Eudora was engaged to wed; her fiancé, a shopkeeper named Charles O'Brien. Eventually the couple planned to open a huge emporium there in Ft. Morgan.

Just two weeks later, a letter arrived from Sadie Dooley. Abby was horrified to learn that Ethan Tuttle had been robbed and murdered after leaving the Honey Belle, shortly after he purchased the Two-Crow's land. Pete Black, another Honey Belle regular was hanged for the crime. Madam Laycock refused to believe in his guilt.

The job in the hotel kitchen remained unpleasant and trying. Still, over a year had passed and Abby had managed to keep the position.

Diligently, she was decorating a platter of pastries as an excited waiter dashed amongst the kitchen staff.

"Guess who is sitting in my station!" he enthused. "Mrs. Darien Birkshire, Meredith Birkshire!"

"Well, la-de-da! The old dowager herself," exclaimed one of the cooks.

"Who? Who is she?" Abby was curious to know.

"Darien Birkshire was one of the founding fathers of Denver. He came from a prominent family back east. Here, he struck a silver mine. How's that for luck!" Old Meredith is his widow, the chintz–covered bitch!"

"I applied to be her personal maid and cook just two days ago," said another. "Unfortunately, she doesn't want a woman with children, and I have several. Pity. It paid well too, room and board included."

"Where does she live?" Abby inquired.

The cooks howled with laughter. "Only the most exclusive section of town, where else?"

"Her home must be a palace. What does it look like?" Abby persisted.

The following morning Abby sent word to the hotel staff that she was ill. Afterward, she traveled the wide boulevards to search for the most fashionable neighborhood in Denver. She left her children behind, as usual.

Beautifully landscaped lawns with elms, maples, oaks and chestnut trees embraced magnificently vivid gardens. Victorian mansions, one after the other, each more stately and palatial than the one before, filled Abby's senses with admiration and wonderment.

The sprawling Birkshire estate was largely obscured by abundant greenery covering a vast lawn. Abby dismounted the buckboard. She tied the horses at the open front gate, and walked to the mansion. A plump, round-faced maid answered her knock.

Abby swallowed deeply. "I'm here for the position of personal servant to Mrs. Birkshire. Has it been filled?"

Abby was beckoned inside and told to wait. The house was the most splendid and lavish she had ever viewed; grander than the Honey Belle and without the tawdriness.

Nearly three-quarters of an hour passed. Finally, an elderly woman attired in pale chintz appeared at the crest of the staircase. She was tall and slender. Her back firmly erect, she descended the stairs. Abby noticed she used a cane.

The young woman rose to her feet and smiled.

"I expect my servants to curtsy." Mrs. Birkshire glared.

"Well, I'm not your servant. Not yet." Abby politely countered.

"And perhaps you never shall be. Do you have any references?"

"No, but I can get a fine one. The Rev. Thomas Gregory in New Mexico territory. I'm a hard worker, Ma'am."

She looked Abby over beneath a wrinkled nose. "Are you a married lady?"

"I'm a widow, Ma'am."

"Do you have children?"

Abby shook her head. "No," she lied. "I'm recently widowed."

"You'll entertain no gentlemen callers on these grounds, understand?"

Abby lowered her eyes and nodded.

“Eleanor, whom you’ve met, shall be leaving. The position is a special one. I need a companion as well as a servant.” Mrs. Birkshire continued to explain the varied duties and her many expectations.

Abby sensed she had made a dreadful impression upon the worldly old dowager.

“The position is yours. Eleanor will be delighted that she may finally leave.”

“Are there other servants here about?” Abby asked as she glanced about the enormous mansion.

Mrs. Birkshire appeared incredulous. “Certainly, but you shall be the only one to reside on the property. I value my privacy. Naturally, you’ll be expected to wear a uniform.”

Abby was escorted to a room off the carriage house. The living area was small. The décor here was far simpler, with mostly plain oak furniture.

“The bedroom is upstairs in the attic.” Eleanor pointed. “I’ll pack as fast as I’m able and be out of here. My sympathy to you, Miss!”

Abby hurried back to the apartment. Quickly, she gathered up the family’s possessions. “We’ll have to sneak in after 6:00 PM, when the other servants leave,” she told Blaine and Lorella. “Remember, you must be silent, always.”

The abundant foliage on the Birkshire estate was to the family’s advantage, as was the darkness. Abby insisted the curtains be tightly closed at all times. She cautioned the children to remain inside.

Blaine and Lorella slept downstairs in sleeping rolls.

“I can keep watch over you, and be here when you need me,” she assured them. “Blaine, I’m depending on you to keep your baby sister quiet while I’m over in the main house.”

The boy gave her a sour look.

As Abby bathed Lorella, she noticed a rainbow of bruises upon the child’s body. She had found bruises before, but none this severe. Abby inquired as to where they came from.

“Bane!” came the reply.

“Blaine?” Abby was astounded. “Blaine did this?” Furiously she confronted her son.

The boy vehemently denied harming his sister. “She’s clumsy.” He shrugged. “Then she tries to get me in trouble!”

Blaine received a severe whipping from his mother. Afterward, Abby thought of Jovah and felt ashamed.

A month later, Abby was summoned to the upstairs library the moment she reported to work. Mrs. Birkshire was upset and angry.

"Several of my neighbors have reported seeing a dark boy playing among the trees and shrubbery upon these grounds."

"A dark boy?" Abby tried to sound surprised.

"Yes, a dark child, a Mexican perhaps. It you should see him, notify the authorities immediately."

"Uh, certainly."

"As you wish, M'lady! You keep forgetting!" The old woman slammed her cane against a table so forcefully it rattled as if to collapse.

Abby nodded and curtsied. Quickly she backed away. Later she confronted Blaine.

"This is a prison!" he screamed. "At least I was free to go outdoors when we lived in that creaky, little apartment!"

Abby cautioned him to keep his voice down. "You were supposed to be inside watching Lorella."

"I'm no baby's nursemaid! It's torture having to stay here. There's nothing to do! And I hate Denver! It rains almost every afternoon."

"Blaine, quiet, please. Someone may be passing by outside."

"It ain't natural the way we live." Blaine picked up his Bible, the one from the Rev. Gregory. Angrily, he flung it across the room. "I'll die here if we stay!"

Abby retrieved the Holy Book. She handed it to Blaine. "Repent your temper. This situation is only temporary. Someday we'll own a house with a vegetable garden, and a few chickens. And maybe I can take in sewing, too. But right now I need this position to make that possible."

The following day, Abby bought Blaine a red toy wagon and Lorella a large doll dressed in lace.

"This is a baby's toy!" Blaine complained. "I'm ten years old! You bought the milksop two gifts."

Abby refused to argue. Exasperated, she turned her back and went upstairs. A second later, she heard Lorella screaming. As she rushed back down, she caught Blaine tugging mightily upon the child's tresses. She rebuked him severely.

The following Christmas, Abby bought both children an abundance of toys and gifts she could barely afford. Now they will both have plenty to occupy their time inside, she thought hopefully.

As soon as summer arrived, Abby often noticed Blaine sneaking out the window into the darkness of the night. He loved to climb the oak trees and take shelter in their branches. Abby took sympathy upon him, and said nothing.

Early in the fall, Lorella awoke crying from a nightmare. Abby hastened downstairs to comfort her. Blaine was unable to climb back inside quickly enough. His mother was forced to scold him. The boy cursed his sister viciously.

Slowly, another year passed. Mrs. Birkshire complained of hearing children's voices on the property. Abby insisted she had heard nothing.

After tidying up for the evening, Abby hurried home to the carriage house. As she stood hotly rebuking Blaine and Lorella, she was interrupted by a loud knocking on the door.

All three of them froze, their bodies tense. The knocking persisted. Soon it became a determined pounding. Abby instructed the children to quietly run upstairs and hide. She took a deep, nervous breath before answering the door.

The man who stood before her was not immediately recognizable, until she noticed the lewd smile and expression. Slick Larsen! His face was broader and more deeply furrowed, his dirty-blonde hair thinner. However, his large muscular frame was fuller and more powerful now.

# Chapter Eight

Abby gasped. “Slick Larsen!”

Quickly, Slick pushed her aside as he swaggered into the room.

“What are you doing here? What do you want?” Abby demanded to know.

“Your man Jovah owed me $500.”

“Take it up with Jovah. He’s not here!”

“Yeah, I know. Jovah’s dead.”

“What? No! No, he ain’t. He took off.”

Larsen glared at her askance. He snorted, and chortled. “Two-Crows and I were blood brothers. Now he would never up and take off without first saying something to me.”

“He couldn’t pay your price Slick. That’s why he left.”

“No, he wouldn’t do that. He owed me more than money.”

Slick looked her over suspiciously. “What did you do? Kill him in his sleep? Then left his remains up in the hills for the animals?”

“No. Jovah abandoned me. I swear!”

“Yeah, sure, and maggots turn into butterflies. Just pay me and I’ll vamoose. I’ve been carrying your debt for many moons now. I figure with interest you owe me at least $2000.”

“$2000! I’m a servant. I can never pay that!”

“Well, I’ll just linger around until you can. It’s almost winter. I need a cozy place like this.”

“Get out! Blaine, go fetch the authorities! Bring them here.”

The boy emerged from the attic.

“Go ahead, son. But be prepared to see your mother hang. By the way, does the old bitch over in the big house know you have children?”

“Of course she does,” Abby said.

“Strange, I applied for a job on your day off and was told none were allowed on the property. Seems she enjoys quiet.”

“Mrs. Birkshire adores my children,” Abby lied.

“I’m sure. They’ll keep me company while you’re slaving like a donkey to repay my loan.”

Larsen made the downstairs couch his bed. It was actually too short and narrow for him. Also he complained it was lumpy.

Often he would remove a large, antique-gold watch from his pocket. It appeared familiar. Now Abby remembered. Ethan Tuttle!

Months passed, Abby and the children were constantly on edge.

"Why don't you just leave? You'll never collect that amount from me," Abby told him. "I don't have money like that."

"The old lady does. That, and a lot more. You and I could live like royalty down in old Mexico."

Abby refused to hear any more. She had to find a way to force Larsen to leave. He possessed a malevolent aura. The children were terrified of him.

Often he disappeared for the day and would sneak back after dark. Abby prayed he would lose interest in his scheme and move on. However, as long as his possessions remained, that was unlikely.

Aunt Eudora and her new husband Charles O'Brien had comfortably settled in Ft. Morgan. They were eager for a visit. Abby continually made excuses to keep them away.

Late one evening when Slick returned, he produced a jar of grey-green powder. "I purchased this from a Chinaman, swore it was undetectable." Larsen grinned. "It'll take care of the old lady."

Abby was horrified. She ordered Slick to remove it from the premises.

"You're in my debt." He bristled. "With interest, you owe me another couple thousand. Well, I'll deduct some for food and lodging. So let's keep it an even $2000."

He placed the jar before her. "Just add a pinch to each meal, the old bitch will start taking ill. While she's laid up, we'll start cleaning her out. After we're finished, give her the rest of the jar. She'll be finished too." He smirked.

"Mrs. Birkshire owes you nothing!" Abby snarled.

"You help mine the gold, I'll erase your debt." He belched. "One way or another I'm getting what's owed."

"No, I could never do such a thing to anyone."

"Hey! No one knows you're keeping young'uns here. If they were to up and vanish one day, it wouldn't matter."

"You harm them, and I'll take my chances with the authorities. You hear me!"

Abby knew she could never harm Mrs. Birkshire. She continued to stall Larsen in spite of his almost constant pressure.

Fond as he was of liquor, Larsen liked to keep his wits around the family. "I don't want you murdering me in my sleep, the way you did Jovah." he frequently told Abby.

However, one particularly cold evening he brought back a bottle of whiskey. He insisted on sharing it with her. "We'll get drunk together."

Indignant, Abby refused.

Slick grabbed her by the hair, and began forcing it down her throat. Abby began to choke. She fought back. Blaine hurried to the rescue.

Angrily, Slick turned. He struck the boy so hard with his fist, Blaine was knocked unconscious. Lorella looked on as if in a stupor.

"You're exactly like Jovah!" Abby screamed. "No wonder you were so fond of each other!" She darted toward her son.

Larsen intercepted her. "You're giving me what's owed." He leered lecherously. What juicy techniques did you learn at the Honey Belle Saloon? Let's go upstairs and find out."

Slick yelled in pain as Abby sunk her teeth deep into his wrist. Freed, she raced upstairs to the safety of her bedroom with its tight lock. There, she would retrieve the Colt 45.

Cursing, Slick charged after her. His mind preoccupied, he did not see the toy wagon near the top step. His foot gave way from under him. His arms flailed wildly. He crashed at the bottom of the stairs, his head striking the sharp edge of a brick mantle. Slick's skull cracked open, spilling blood and brains across the floor.

Lorella began shrieking. Before Abby could stop her, she raced wailing and screaming out across the lawn and into the arms of a stranger on the street.

The authorities were summoned. Abby was arrested. She remained jailed without news. Abby constantly inquired as to the whereabouts of her children. No one would comment or speak of them. At last, she was disheartened to tears to learn Blaine and Lorella had been sent to an orphanage.

"Larsen murdered a man back in Durango," Abby told the sheriff. "A fellow called Ethan Tuttle. Pete Black, an innocent man, was hanged for the crime.

The old lawman glared at her suspiciously. "You mean you and Larsen killed Ethan Tuttle together, don't' you?"

"No!" Abby protested. "Tuttle was my friend and my neighbor. He purchased land from me."

"And Larsen was your lover! He was flagrantly living with you, right before your children."

"No! He was threatening our lives. Slick slept on the couch downstairs. I swear!"

The sheriff shook his head in amusement.

Someone entered. Mrs. Birkshire stood regally in the doorway.

"I've come to fetch the prisoner."

"She'll be my guest for a spell longer, I suspect," the sheriff said. "Murder, and the woman was reeking of whiskey when we arrested her." He rolled his eyes in disgust.

The old lady handed him an official looking document.

He appeared befuddled. "Are you certain this is what you want?" he asked in disbelief.

"Are you implying I don't know my own mind?" she snapped, slamming the metal tip of her cane on the floor.

Sheepishly, the sheriff pulled forth his keys and proceeded to unlock Abby's cell.

Mrs. Birkshire stepped forward. "Your buckboard is loaded and waiting outside, along with those two guttersnipes of yours. Here are the wages to which you are entitled." She forcefully shoved the cash into Abby's chest. "Through my influence, I managed to get the case dropped. Of course, I expect you to leave Denver, never to return."

"Mrs. Birkshire, I'm forever indebted to you."

"I didn't do it for you!" the old woman screeched. "I value my privacy as others value gold. I had no desire to be submerged in a scandal. You deceived me from our first encounter. Women of your caliber are trash, filth!" She spat viciously into Abby's face. "Now leave! Flee to some rat's nest among your own kind." She glowered contemptuously.

Hastily, Abby departed. Outside, Blaine and Lorella waited atop the buckboard. A servant stood by the horses, a man she knew only as Ludlow. The tall, long-nosed fellow wrinkled his sallow face in disgust as she took the reins from his hand.

"Where are we going Mama?" Blaine asked as Lorella looked on curiously.

"Ft. Morgan. You've never met your great-aunt Eudora. And I'll be meeting her husband Charles for the first time."

Abby and children were greeted warmly and enthusiastically by the O'Brien couple. The house was homey and comfortable, but not large enough for the extra people.

"I've imposed long enough," Abby said after a few days.

"You're no imposition, you're kinfolk," Eudora explained.

"Sometimes kinfolk are the worst kind." Abby smiled. "We should really be on our way."

"At least wait until winter's end. A young family shouldn't be traveling through snow and ice. It's too perilous," Mr. O'Brien added. He offered her a sales job.

Abby agreed to wait until spring, or the end of the snowfall, whichever came first. A May snowstorm delayed their departure longer than planned.

Charles O'Brien intended to promote Abby at his emporium, while Eudora offered to help the family find living quarters in town.

Abby refused. "There's too many Yankee soldiers here in Ft. Morgan for comfort. I don't like the way they stare at us. Besides, I hear Wyoming territory is mighty impressive."

As the family was loading their possessions, Eudora took Abby aside. "You three are all the kin we have. Charles and I want you to have this." She folded currency into Abby's hand. "We'll miss you all so much. Lorella is the prettiest child I've ever seen. Wish I could raise her as my own."

"We'll return for visits," Abby promised.

Eudora sighed forlornly. "Wyoming is so far away."

Abby steered the buckboard on a northeasterly course. The children were eager to reach the new territory. Days passed, miles were covered. Before long, they approached a serene and scenic little town. The family camped on the wild outskirts for several days.

When it came time to depart, Blaine and Lorella refused.

"We want to build a house right here," Lorella said.

"But we're still in Colorado. What about Wyoming territory?" their mother inquired.

"We found home. We don't need to go anyplace else," Blaine stated matter-of-factly.

"Yes, I believe this is indeed the most beautiful spot we could ever hope for," Abby agreed, as she glanced about.

They stood amidst a lush meadow among chestnut and evergreen trees. Beside them ran a winding brook flowing from a waterfall. Beyond were flowery pastures and dark forests with soft glades. Snow-capped peaks loomed in the distance.

Abby saddled a horse and headed for town. Blaine and Lorella were left behind. Many hours later she returned with welcome news.

"I purchased a cabin a half mile from this spot. The town is called Gideon. I found an opening for a clerk's position at the General Store. The boss seems a fair man. His name is Kale MacDoonan."

Abby took the children to their new home. The cabin was small and Spartan, but at least better than an old miner's shack. The surrounding area was certainly more beautiful.

"I remember something Jovah once said," Abby murmured. "Something about how one must endure the ordeals of purgatory to truly appreciate paradise."

"My papa said that?" Lorella exclaimed.

Blaine scowled. "I don't like remembering that man."

Abby suddenly felt guilty and embarrassed bringing the name up. "If you believe in God strongly enough and pray with conviction, God answers prayers," she explained.

"My prayer was answered. I have my own room. I ain't a nursery maid anymore," Blaine said.

"You'll have the entire cabin to yourself before long. In a few weeks Lorella will be starting school," his mother told him. "She'll leave with me in the mornings and we'll return together late afternoon."

"You never sent me to school!" he hollered. "I'm almost twelve years old!"

"I taught you myself. You would have been uncomfortable in a classroom, Blaine." Abby pointed out.

"But Lorella won't need to worry, will she?" the boy hissed.

"Good lord, Blaine!" Abby tossed up her hands. "Why can't you ever let us be happy? Lord knows I've always done the best I could for you. Why are you always whining?"

Sullen and angry, the boy stormed away. Darkness had fallen. Blaine disappeared into the wilderness. Abby decided to let him be. She and Lorella had supper alone.

Abby felt her son's pain. Her daughter's blue eyes and fair skin would allow her a life forever inaccessible to Blaine. No wonder he seemed to hate the girl at times.

Abby found the clerk's position a far more agreeable occupation than many of her previous ones. The school year soon began. After classes had ended for the day, Lorella would join her mother at MacDoonan's General Store. The little girl helped stock merchandise as well as dust and sweep the floor.

Kale MacDoonan was delighted with the arrangement. "Mrs. MacDoonan lives in that small, wood house out back. She has no interest in shop work," he told them.

Winter came to Gideon. Abby found herself wishing the cabin was closer to town. But isolation was important. Lorella had been instructed never to speak of Blaine. Often she complained of being unable to bring friends home. Again the guilt cut through Abby like a soldier's rapier.

Due to extreme cold and an oncoming blizzard, Mr. MacDoonan allowed Abby to leave work early. As she and Lorella approached their property, suddenly they heard gunfire.

Abby began to sweat in the cold. Her heart raced. She reached for the old Hawken rifle in the back of the buckboard. She ordered Lorella down, before cracking the whip over the horses. They took off at full run toward the cabin.

The place appeared abandoned. Gunfire continued in the wilderness beyond. Heart pounding, Abby followed the sounds on foot. As the shooting ceased, she came to a clearing in the wilderness. Blaine was busily loading the Colt 45.

"Put that down!" she hollered. "It's not a toy, son."

Startled, he jumped in surprise. "And I'm not a boy anymore," he hollered back.

"Yes, you are. Now give me that weapon!"

"Let me have the rifle then. I'm tired of catching game in snares. Besides, it's about time I learned to use a six-shooter."

"Perhaps in another year or two."

"But I'm already a crack shot! Watch the tip of that tree branch." Instantly it was snapped off by a 45 slug.

Abby snatched the gun from Blaine's hand. "Get inside. A storm is coming."

The harsh winter was drawing to a close. As Abby was stocking cans, she noticed a man enter MacDoonan's. He was tall and strongly built. His dark hair displayed graying temples. His jaw was firm. Kale MacDoonan rushed to greet him. The shopkeeper seemed overly obsequious.

“There’s some new merchandise in the store, I see,” the man said, motioning toward Abby.

She pretended not to hear and smiled over toward them.

“That’s Abigail Crowe. She’s a widow woman from Ft. Morgan.”

“I’ll have to stop sending my hired hands over and start coming in myself.”

At that moment Lorella raced in, her school books in tow. She darted behind the counter, next to Abby.

“Hand me up the cans, baby,” her mother instructed.

“My God, is this beautiful child yours?” the man spoke to Abby at last.

“Indeed she is,” Abby declared with pride.

“There’s little resemblance to you. I mean, she’s a different type. Yours is a fair beauty, as was my wife’s. I’m a widower. My name’s Jess Atkinhead.”

He chatted pleasantly with Abby, nearly forgetting his purpose for entering the store. She was flattered by his attention. But something inside of her held back.

“Say, why don’t I take you and your little girl to dinner later,” he offered. “We’ll go to Hettie’s. It’s much better than the Inn.”

Abby hesitated. “Oh, not tonight. Some other time for certain. But please give me more notice, all right?”

Atkinhead appeared puzzled, as well as visibly disappointed. He gathered up his supplies, bid farewell to MacDoonan, and departed. She hoped she didn’t sound impolite.

“You’re a fool,” Kale MacDoonan told her. “I’ll bet Atkinhead owns half of Colorado, or damn near. Every woman in six territories has thrown herself at him.”

Abby did not see Jess Atkinhead again until almost the next winter. She had already forgotten him by the time he showed up at the store. He appeared uncharacteristically shy.

“Is tomorrow evening agreeable?” he asked. “I’d be pleased if you’d dine with me, your little girl, too.”

“Lorella and I will be looking forward to it.” Abby smiled warmly.

Hettie’s was far from a fancy eating establishment. Jesse swore the fare was unsurpassed. Abby was unable to get Blaine out of her thoughts. The boy would be responsible for cooking his own supper. She recalled the seething anger on his face when she told him.

However, Abby was weary of always feeling short-changed. She was tired of Blaine's constant complaining and his whining. Still, his festering rage and resentment over-shadowed everything.

"Hettie Wheaton cooks better than a New Orleans chef." Jess winked at a plump woman in a soiled apron as she passed by.

She giggled daintily as a coquette. Abby's train of thought was broken. She forced a smile.

After the meal, Jess insisted upon accompanying Abby and Lorella home on horseback. Abby told him she wasn't defenseless and pretended to be indignant. Eventually, Jess went on his way and Abby breathed a sigh of relief.

As she and Lorella returned to the cabin, Blaine was in a predictably foul and tetchy mood. Abby refused to fuss. More work awaited her at home and she was already tired.

As soon as his mother's back was turned, Blaine struck Lorella hard enough to leave a throbbing, scarlet imprint on her face. The child cried for the rest of the evening. Abby fought the urge to beat Blaine.

Atkinhead began showing up more frequently at the General Store.

"Jess is now purchasing items he'll never even use," Kale MacDoonan told her. Jokingly, he begged Abby never to leave his employment.

Throughout the winter and spring, Abby and her small daughter frequently enjoyed dinner with Jess Atkinhead at Hettie's. When summer arrived and the school year ended, Lorella remained home with Blaine. Abby and Jess now dined alone.

"Your daughter is awful young to be left on her own way out in the wilderness all day," Jess remarked with concern.

"I have help," Abby replied, without going into detail.

"Actually I prefer it this way." His eyes gleamed. "After my Elisabeth passed on, I never expected to find anyone as special again."

Abby felt suddenly uncomfortable. "Please don't get serious over me, Jess. There's so much ugliness in my past. So much you could never understand."

"Lady, I live in the present. The past is gone. We determine our own futures. But first, we must lay the past to rest."

"But Jess, you still grieve for Elisabeth. I can see it. How did she die?"

"Pneumonia. She was born in the Bayou country of Louisiana. She had no tolerance for Colorado winters."

"Yes, I was born in Texas. I was almost claimed by pneumonia myself once."

Jess reached for Abby's hand. She pulled away.

"I can't help remembering my husband. He saved me, only to enslave me."

"You can't allow bad experiences to blacken your future happiness." Jess told her.

"Sometimes it's impossible," Abby exclaimed in exasperation.

"No, no, nothing between us is impossible or unforgivable. Whatever hard luck you've known in the past is over. I'm seeing to that personally. After all, you've ended my sorrow."

"Jess, you are a godsend." Abby sighed.

"So, when are you inviting me out to your place for a home-cooked meal? I've never tasted your cooking. What's the problem? Can't you cook or are you hiding another beau out there?" He winked.

# Chapter Nine

Abby could not delay any longer. After much agonizing, she decided it was time Blaine and her suitor finally met. Jess Atkinhead was invited to supper. Abby found herself anxious and on edge all day.

Lorella was setting the table. Abby was preoccupied cooking a large slab of meat.  There came the knocking at the door. Before his mother realized it, Blaine swung the door wide open. Jess was early.

Jess and the boy stood face to face. Abby felt guilty for not preparing Atkinhead. The dismay and displeasure in his eyes was unmistakable.

He glowered down at Blaine, "What's a little buck like you doing here?" he snarled.

Abby raced to the child's side. "This is my son! My first born."

"You mean you actually let a savage touch you?" Jess winced. "And you birthed another redskin? This thing?"

"My child is no thing! You'd better go, Jess. You're no longer welcome here." There was a sadness as well as anger in her voice.

"I actually mistook you for being decent. I sure was one plum fool, and a blind mooncalf." Jess shook his head forlornly.

"The mistake was mine. Now get off my property!" Abby demanded.

"Get the peacemaker, Mama! I'll get rid of him," Blaine interjected.

"No, Mr. Atkinhead is leaving."

The following morning Abby dreaded going into town. Mr. MacDoonan prodded her with questions about dinner with Jess. Even the reclusive Mrs. MacDoonan put in an appearance to assuage her curiosity.

Abby merely told them her personal association with the man was over. She figured they would hear the details from Atkinhead soon enough. Again, she would be shunned.

Several days passed. Abby was busy attending to customers when she noticed Jess enter the store. He pretended to be looking over merchandise and refused MacDoonan's service. After her customers departed, Jess approached Abby. He was unable to look her in the eye.

"I behaved like an addle-brained jackass the other evening," he murmured.

"You certainly did," Abby agreed.

"I don't want to lose you Abby. I'd like to discuss a matter of importance. It won't wait. Please come with me. Now."

"Go on ahead. It's a nice day. I'm giving you the afternoon off." Mr. MacDoonan waved them away.

Jess extended his arm to Abby. He led her to a waiting buggy outside. They rode for miles.

Eventually they came upon a twelve acre lake; its water the color of polished turquoise. A vast cherry orchard in full blossom surrounded it. Snow-capped mountains loomed in the distance.

"This is Lake Elisabeth," Jess announced with pride. "My favorite place in all creation."

"The territory is abundant in beauty." Abby smiled.

"You belong here with me," he declared. "I'll provide well for your children. I want to send them to a private school back east. An excellent education would give them hope for the future."

Abby stammered for an answer. "I…I don't know Jess. I'd first have to discuss it with Blaine and Lorella."

He grasped Abby, pulling her tightly against his chest. "Honestly, it would be in their best interests, and ours."

Abby's arms encircled him. Her lips parted as Jess kissed them fervently and repeatedly. Her fingers softly stroked his back. Jess began unfastening the top buttons of her blouse as he kissed wetly down her neck.

"After the children are away, you can come work for me on my ranch. I'll give you a feigned title like head-maid or head-cook. Of course you'll never do actual work."

"What? Jess! No!"

"If that's not agreeable, I'll build you a house on my property. Perhaps right here. We can rendezvous whenever we desire."

Aghast, Abby shoved Jess away as she jumped from the buggy. "I actually believed you brought me out here to propose marriage."

Jess jumped down after her. "Marriage! I couldn't defile the memory of Elisabeth with a squaw woman by my side."

With those hated words Abby slapped Atkinhead furiously across his face. "No, you just want a squaw woman by your side in bed!"

Jess seized Abby firmly by the arm. "It's the best offer your kind is ever going to get."

"Well, no thank you!" She struck him in the face with her fist, nearly knocking him to the ground, as she pulled away.

"You ain't getting haughty with me, you redskin–birthing, squaw bitch!" He lunged at her from the back.

Abby was thrust face first onto the ground. Before she could rise, Jess was atop her. As he turned her over, she slugged him with all her might. Enraged, Atkinhead slugged her back.

Abby lay unconscious for a few seconds. When she awoke, Jess was ripping off her clothes. Gritting her teeth, she tore mightily into the flesh of his face and neck with her fingernails.

He cried out. Jess struck her brutally again. She felt him dragging her into the lush thicket among the cherry trees. Abby resisted. Jess began striking her repeatedly.

Night was falling when she regained consciousness again. The air was growing cold. Abby attempted to cover herself with the remains of her torn clothes. Jess and the buggy had long since departed. Humiliated, she started home on foot.

Through the darkness, time and miles passed tediously. Bears and mountain lions could be heard in the distance. Strangely, Abby was unafraid. Death would have been a welcome blessing, she thought. No, Abby shook herself, she must survive.

At that moment she heard Blaine's voice echoing through the darkness. Or was it her imagination? Abby hollered out. She dropped to her knees from exhaustion.

A light emerged through the woods. Abby pulled herself to her feet. Blaine was on horseback with a lantern.

As he approached, she saw the horror reflected in his eyes. She must have appeared a bloodied walking corpse.

"Jesse Atkinhead attacked me!" she screamed.

"What were you doing with him?" Blaine asked in astonishment.

"Never mind. We must fetch the law."

Blaine took his mother home. Abby gave him directions to Sheriff Connor's office.

"Our secret is out, or will be soon. Jess must be forced to pay for what he did." Abby was adamant.

The lawman Connor was annoyed at being wakened from sleep, and having to make the journey way out to the cabin at that hour. He listened patiently to Abby, but showed little concern.

"I'll ride out to the Atkinhead place tomorrow," he assured her.

"Tomorrow!" she exclaimed. "You must go tonight and arrest him."

"I'm not arresting anyone until I hear both sides. Now get some sleep. I'll send Doc out here come morning."

Abby and Blaine watched him ride away. Lorella had fallen back to sleep.

"I'll go take care of Atkinhead, Mama," Blaine asserted. "I'll put a 45 slug in him. That will even both our scores."

"No, we're not savages. I took the law into my own hands once before, never again. We'll let the sheriff deal with him."

Several days passed before Abby felt well enough to make the journey into town. Her first stop was the sheriff's office.

"What do you mean, you're not arresting Atkinhead!" she screamed, "You know what was done to me."

"Well, Jess tells it differently," Sheriff Connor explained. "He claims it was consensual. You seduced him, expecting him to marry you. After you found out he wouldn't you lost your temper. Jess claims you went wild and attacked him! And he has the bloody wounds to prove it!"

"That's a god-damn lie! He attacked me! Look at my wounds compared to his. My word is truth and I'm pressing charges."

The sheriff sighed as he shook his head. "Then I suggest you hire yourself a lawyer. You'll need a good one."

Indignantly, Abby departed. Her next stop was MacDoonan's General Store. Kale returned her greeting with a half-hearted nod. He remained unusually silent and seemed uncomfortable in her presence.

"I'll start unloading those crates out back today," she volunteered.

"Abby, wait." His voice was high and strained. He appeared nervous.

"What's wrong, Kale?"

"I'm truly sorry." He took a deep shaky breath. "But I won't be needing you anymore. Money is too tight here right now."

"Sure, Kale." She sighed with disgust. "I'm not surprised. You lick Jess Atkinhead's backside just like everyone else." Abby slammed the door on her way out.

She knew her next stop. A wire was sent to Ft. Morgan. Later she received word the O'Briens were sending help. Lorella was pulled from school. Abby began tutoring her at home with Blaine.

"I don't have a job anymore," she told them. "Just as long as we tend garden and there is fresh game we won't starve."

Several weeks passed. Abby and Lorella were busy with laundry when they heard a rider approach. It was a strange looking man in a suit and small hat. Blaine raced from the house with the Hawken rifle.

"Are you Abigail Crowe?" the man called out.

Hesitantly, she answered.

"Thank goodness!" he exclaimed. "I thought I was lost. No one would give me directions to this place."

"I'm Clayton Faraday, attorney-at-law. The O'Brien's hired me. They're arriving as soon as business allows."

Abby yanked the rifle away from Blaine. Politely, she invited Faraday inside.

"Permit me to be forthright, Mrs. Crowe. Your case is weak. It's Atkinhead's word against yours. I was at his ranch yesterday. He insists what happened was basically a sweetheart's quarrel gone awry."

"What? He's a damn liar!"

"That will be difficult to prove in court," Faraday confessed. "From what I've learned already, most of the citizens of Gideon knew that you and Jess were keeping close romantic company."

"We courted, sure, but that's all," Abby swore.

"Many are already saying that you're just vengeful and bitter because you schemed to marry Jess Atkinhead. A trial would prove deeply embarrassing to you."

"Mr. Faraday, don't you understand? A serious wrong was committed here. I can't allow him to get away with it; otherwise I could never respect myself."

"I'm just trying to prepare you for the ordeal you're going to face in court, Mrs. Crowe. Atkinhead has already retained a formidable attorney, Alexander Osbourne. The man is Harvard educated. And his brother-in-law yet!"

Clayton Faraday took up temporary residence at the Inn. Several more weeks passed. Faraday informed Abby the trial would begin November 30, circuit judge Benjamin Hardstone presiding.

"November 30$^{th}$!" she exclaimed. "But that's months away! Snow will be falling."

"Unfortunately, that's to Atkinhead's advantage. The more time that passes, the colder the incident will become," he lamented.

When fall arrived, Charles and Eudora O'Brien came from Ft. Morgan. Blaine managed to snare three pheasants and two ducks for the occasion. A large dinner celebration awaited their reunion. Faraday was also a guest. He arrived late.

"Atkinhead is offering you several thousand dollars to drop the charges," he told Abby. "Perhaps it would be wise to consider it."

"No amount of money is worth that!" Abby hollered. I'm doing this to preserve my dignity. He must go to trial."

Faraday glanced at Blaine and Lorella. "Atkinhead is having you investigated. Any indiscretions in your past are likely to become public."

Abby felt suddenly queasy. "I can't back down now; Jess has to be made to suffer for what he did, at my expense if necessary."

Eudora remained at the cabin with the family. She and Abby shared a bed. Charles returned to the Inn with Clayton Faraday. The two men occupied a room together.

Abby slept little, and when she did, her slumber was permeated with nightmares. Anxiety caused her frequent illness. Eudora was forced to perform most of the chores, plus tend to the family besides. But she never complained.

As the trial date finally came, Abby found herself strangely relieved, in spite of the ordeal she knew was awaiting her.

She studiously observed as attorneys Faraday and Osbourne interviewed the jurors; Most were sodbusters, or sodbuster's wives, who only knew Jessimyn Atkinhead by name.

These were strong-backed, hard-working, Christian people similar to her and her parents. Abby felt comforted and reassured by their presence.

Faraday was graceful in his actions. He presented the case with confidence and aplomb. Abby began to feel at ease. She was sworn in.

However, as she related the incident to the jurors. She began to choke back tears. As she described the attack, in realistic detail, the jury and courtroom seemed transfixed in fascination. The quietude felt oppressive and suffocating to Abby.

Alexander Osbourne approached the stand. To Abby's surprise, he was initially sympathetic and friendly, but soon that abruptly ended.

"On the afternoon in question, you methodically seduced Mr. Jessimyn Atkinhead with the hope of luring, or should I say snaring him into matrimony. Is that not true, Mrs. Two-Crows? Your actual name is Two-Crows, and not Crowe, am I correct?"

"Yes, but the rest is untrue. I swear to God! Jess forced himself on me!"

"But that is only your word, Mrs. Two-Crows. Were you not married to a half-breed in Durango, inside a saloon yet, where you had been employed for several years? You've already lied about your name and your past. How can you expect anyone to believe you now?"

"Because it's the truth!" Abby expostulated. "I was a seamstress at the saloon, not a whore!"

"You think us all fools, ma'am? And what about the Muddycreek mining camp? You shared a tent with a well-known whore by the name of Mariposa Jones. The two of you worked the camp together."

Faraday protested Osbourne's line of questioning to the judge. "These matters are irrelevant and prejudicial," he insisted.

However the judge over-ruled him. Osbourne was instructed to proceed.

"Mrs. Two-Crows, is it not true you spent jail time in Denver for the murder of one Slick Larsen, your lover?"

"Slick was never my lover. His death was an accident."

"But you and Mr. Larsen were living clandestinely in sin, at the time of his death, in the presence of your two children. Is that not true, also?"

"He slept downstairs, not in my bed! Slick was threatening me, and my young'uns."

"Mr. Larsen possessed a considerable and reprehensible illicit reputation with a history of thievery and violence beginning in his childhood. When did you first meet this man, Mrs. Two-Crows?"

Abby paused to think. "Many years ago back in Durango. He was a friend to my husband."

"You mean your husband, the half-breed, named Jovah Two-Crows? What became of this man, your husband?"

Abby took a deep breath. She realized she must remain in control. "He up and left me. I don't know what became of him," she lied.

"It is odd indeed that after your husband deserted you, as you say, no one has ever heard or seen anything of Jovah Two-Crows again. Not a trace remains of him anywhere! It is just as if he's evaporated into the evening mist. Wouldn't you agree that's strange and suspicious?"

"I don't know," Abby's voice was strained. "He's no longer part of my life."

"Could it be that you and your lover, Slick Larsen, murdered the half-breed Two-Crows?"

Faraday vociferously protested. “This is merely malicious speculation, your honor.”

For once, the protest was sustained. Abby was visibly relieved. Her reputation sullied, Osbourne continued to assail her mercilessly about her alleged scheme to ensnare Jess Atkinhead.

Abby was mentally and physically exhausted as the long day drew to an end. Wearily, she stepped from the stand. Faraday cautioned her that she may be recalled later for further questioning.

“We must send a wire to Durango immediately. Sadie Dooley and Madam Honey Laycock will prove to everyone that I was never a whore,” she insisted.

The following morning, Kale MacDoonan was subpoenaed as a reluctant witness for the prosecution. Directly afterward, Jess Atkinhead took the stand.

He carried himself with refinement and self-assurance, his demeanor dignified and affable. Often, he would smile warmly at the jurors, as if these twelve strangers were dear friends.

“Yes, I eagerly courted Miss Abigail,” he admitted. “As you can all see, she is quite a fetching woman.”

“Did you ever intend to marry her?” Osbourne asked.

Jess paused a full sixty seconds before he spoke. “No, but I blame myself for putting that idea into her head. I’m a widower. Abigail was the first woman since my wife Elisabeth with whom I could fully open myself. I confided my grief and loneliness to her. Apparently, she read more into my soul bearing than was intended.”

“Mrs. Two-Crows attempted to use this to her advantage,” his attorney stated.

“I hate to believe such things of anyone, especially someone who seemed as compassionate as Abby.”

Clayton Faraday objected. The objection was sustained. He approached the stand.

“Mr. Atkinhead, the day of the alleged incident, we’ve already established that you, in fact, went to MacDoonan’s General Store to call upon the widow Crowe. Why did you insist upon taking her way out to an isolated spot upon your property? What was your intent?”

“My intent was to spare Abby undue embarrassment. I wanted to sever our relationship in privacy, in case of any tears or feminine histrionics.”

"But Mr. Atkinhead, that was unnecessary, since Abigail Crowe had already ended the relationship several days before. In fact she had ordered you off her property. Is that not correct?"

"Actually her red-skinned son didn't like my face and threatened to blow it off with a six-shooter. It was at that moment I realized we could no longer continue our relationship."

"After you took Mrs. Crowe out to Lake Elisabeth what did you say to her? What were your exact words?"

A sly half-smile crept over Jess's face. "As I recall, we spent little time in conversation. She behaved like a lioness in heat and I was the astonished prey."

"Oh, so you're saying the lady seated there overpowered you?"

"No, I'm saying she surprised me. Delightfully so."

The courtroom erupted in laughter, titters, and chortles. The judge banged his gavel to restore calm.

"And why would my client behave in such a manner, especially after the ugly words that ensued between you several days earlier?"

"Abby was expecting a marriage proposal. She admitted this to me during our intimate encounter. After she learned I had no such intent, she became furious. Spurned, Abby turned into a wildcat!" Jess unbuttoned his collar. He pointed out lined scars on his face and neck.

"Why did you offer to have Mrs. Crowe's two children educated back east with you paying all the expenses?" Was it to have them out of the way so you could take their mother into your home as your mistress?"

Not surprisingly, Jess denied all of this.

"It was you who was spurned, and not her!" Faraday hollered."You're accustomed to having your own way, aren't you? So you attacked her brutally and forced yourself upon her."

Alexander Osbourne protested. The protest was sustained. Jess Atkinhead stepped down from the stand. Court adjourned for the day.

The temperature dropped to zero as howling, icy blizzards lasted for days. Snow drifts were so deep court was postponed for two weeks. The family was forced to take up residence at the Inn.

"This is to our advantage," Abby told Faraday. "Have you heard yet from Madam Laycock or Sadie Dooley in Durango?" she asked hopefully.

Clayton Faraday glanced down at his shoes. "Two summers ago, Sadie Dooley took on a job sewing costumes for a traveling troupe of actors. She left no forwarding address. They believe she's somewhere down in Venezuela at the moment."

"As for Honey Laycock, she doesn't want to get entangled in this. Many of her most prized customers are either good friends or do business with Jess Atkinhead. She hopes you understand."

"Yes, I suppose I do. To a whore, money comes first," Abby said bitterly.

A week before Christmas the trial resumed. To Abby's relief, she was not called to testify again. But neither was Jess Atkinhead. Instead, came a string of character witnesses from four territories; men and women who swore Atkinhead was honorable and upstanding beyond reproach.

Finally came the closing arguments from the two attorneys. Faraday referred to Abby as a devout Christian, as were the jury members themselves, a woman who had struggled with a hard life, as they had surely done.

Jessimyn Atkinhead was portrayed as a man who had created a successful life and became wealthy by the exploitation of such persons with little regard for them.

Abby strongly identified with the jurors. She hoped they would relate to her anguish, and see through Jess Atkinhead's lies.

Alexander Osbourne arose and prepared to speak. He sniffed and cleared his throat as he paced before the jury box. "Our evidence has already revealed that the plaintiff, Abigail Two-Crows, is of questionable character. She has led a sordid and suspicious life."

"She arrived in Gideon not long ago, under the bogus name of Crowe, with her two offspring. Both have Indian blood, one born a bastard. Her intent was to deceive, to ensnare a trusting, law-abiding citizen for her own personal gain. This woman masquerades as a decent Christian, when in fact, she is nothing more than a common calico cat."

The jury remained sequestered for the rest of the day. Abby sat nervously with the O'Briens. Her fingers shook as she reached into her handbag for a handkerchief and mirror. She gazed over at Atkinhead.

He was engaged in animated conversation with his attorney. They appeared to be bantering gaily back and forth. Doesn't he have a conscience? She wondered.

At last the bailiff handed the judge a note. The court was again called to order as the six men and six women re-entered.

# CHAPTER TEN

Judge Hardstone asked Jess Atkinhead to please rise, along with the jury foreman. Abby held her breath. "How do you find the defendant?" the judge asked.

The old, barely-shaven sodbuster cleared his throat. His large Adam's apple bobbed up and down. "We find the defendant, Jessimyn Atkinhead, not guilty, your honor."

Not guilty! Abby was numb with disbelief. Clayton Faraday dropped his gaze. He covered his face with his hands. Devastated, Abby looked over toward the jurors.

How could these people let her down? These were folks exactly like her parents, exactly like friends and neighbors back in Wildwillow.

Exactly, of course! They too had all turned against her in her desperation and need. There was no difference.

A merry mob of boisterous congratulations surrounded Jess Atkinhead. Abby felt the blood draining from her face as she arose. A comforting hand touched her shoulder.

"I'm sorry, but we tried," Aunt Eudora said.

Abby bristled. "If I carried a weapon, I believe I'd murder him this second, the attorney, and that judge, too."

"Keep your voice down," Faraday cautioned.

"Those jurors are fools," Abby snapped.

"Calm yourself, it's over, let's leave."

"We'll all have dinner in town before you go back to the cabin," Charles O'Brien suggested.

"What will you and your family do now?" Faraday asked Abby.

"I'm going to leave. That's for certain! Though I don't know how soon I can sell my place."

"You and the young'uns come back to Ft. Morgan with us," Eudora said.

Wearily, Abby shook her head.

Blaine and Lorella were waiting upstairs at the Inn. After dinner, Abby insisted both O'Briens stay behind with Faraday.

"You need to pack for the journey home," she said.

The cabin seemed particularly chilly and desolate, no longer a place of solace. Silently, Blaine and Lorella went off to bed.

The darkness felt empty and oppressive. Hours passed, Abby tried unsuccessfully to fall asleep. Suddenly, Blaine charged through the bedroom door. "Someone is coming," he whispered with alarm.

Fatigued, Abby sat up to listen. "No, it's a dream, son. Go back to bed."

The loud neigh of a horse outside her bedroom window caused her to rise and investigate. "One of the horses is loose that's all," she assured Blaine. "I'll take care of it. I can't rest anyway."

As Abby entered the main room, she heard a commotion outside. A flicker, then a flash appeared at the south window. Without warning, the glass shattered, almost exploding in myriad pieces. A flaming torch blazed upon the wood floor, less than a yard from her feet.

Abby jumped back as the room instantly shot into flames. She shouted out Lorella's name. The child screamed from an adjoining room. The smoke and flames were already so thick and overpowering Abby could barely maneuver. She shoved Blaine toward the front door.

Eyes stinging and choking for breath, Abby beat back the flames with a throw-rug as she made her way toward Lorella's room. The two escaped through a window.

Blaine waited a safe distance away in the bushes. Voracious tongues of fire crackled and hissed as they consumed the cabin. The garden had been trampled. The chickens were killed or scattered. The horses were gone. The buckboard had been trashed.

The early morning sun found the family shivering in the extreme cold, attired only in nightclothes, huddled together in Lorella's scorched quilt. Eventually all three horses had found their way back.

"That's something to be grateful for," Blaine said.

"We have nothing for which to be grateful," Abby replied.

"What will we do, Mama?"

Abby closed her eyes and sighed deeply. "We're leaving so-called civilization behind. We're going up into the foothills and the mountains. We'll hunt and trap. We can fish and pan for gold."

"That's the way we should have always lived." Blaine's eyes glistened.

Abby gazed down at her daughter, sleeping quietly in her arms.

"First, I'm taking Lorella to Aunt Eudora and Uncle Charles. Your sister is a social creature. She'd die from the isolation where we're going."

The O'Briens were alarmed as they first spied Abby and family waiting in the Inn's lobby. Eudora broke down in tears as she listened to the account of the night before. The family was taken upstairs and provided warm attire.

"Faraday left early this morning," Charles said. "And you're liable to end up murdered here. All of you must leave with us."

"You belong with your kin in Ft. Morgan," Eudora added.

Abby shook her head. "I've had my fill of so-called decent, respectable folks. They're nothing but hypocrites. Blaine and I are eager to depart civilized society," she seethed.

"You won't survive in the wild," Eudora lamented.

"Ten years ago we wouldn't have," Abby said. "I'll sell one of the horses. That'll give us enough cash for necessities. Will you be responsible for selling my land here, Charles?"

He nodded in resignation. "How shall we reach you?"

Abby paused to think. "For the time being, we'll contact you when needed." She knelt down and pulled Lorella tightly to her chest. "I love you, baby. And we'll be seeing you again."

"For God's sake, Abby!" Eudora exclaimed. "Please wait till spring. The weather is too treacherous."

"No, not this time. It must be now." Abby was adamant.

The wilderness offered little comfort. Temperatures fell far below zero. Snow froze, as icicles formed in their hair. Blaine cut long, sturdy poles from tree branches. Abby made a tripod. Blaine then cut almost a dozen smaller poles. The two wedged them all firmly in the earth and lashed them together. After the poles were secure, Abby covered them with antelope hides she had stitched together.

She left a flap open at the top. With these Abby controlled the ventilation with two long interior poles. Inside, they built a fire and covered themselves with bearskins for the night.

"Did you set the traps?" she asked Blaine.

He nodded before drifting to sleep by the flames.

Abby studied her son in the firelight. Blaine was into his teens now. His face was square-jawed as was her own. However, his cheekbones were high and his nose aquiline as was Chief Raging Storm's.

She shuddered at the thought. Blaine was strong and robust, resilient, and resourceful. Abby could see the Apache in him more than ever. Ironically, both were existing as Indians. She forced a sad laugh.

Next day, Blaine stayed behind to check the traps as Abby rode down to the closest trading post. Several days later, she returned with supplies.

Blaine looked her over in disbelief. "What are you wearing?" he exclaimed.

"I should have done this sooner," Abby said as she slid from the horse. "These men's britches are more practical. I told the man at the Trading Post these were for my husband. Doubt he believed me."

Blaine let out a hardy, resounding laugh.

"I brought you a gift." Abby tossed him a six-shooter. "I also picked up a couple of Winchesters. We can't always depend on the traps. We can also pick up mail down at the Trading Post. I sent a letter off to Ft. Morgan."

At last, the snow melted. The sky turned the color of ripe peaches. Mountain flowers blossomed in granite cracks. Mariposa lilies and fragrant wild rose bushes decorated the hillsides amid moss and shrubs.

Abby and Blaine enjoyed their fill of tiny, wild strawberries. Schools of trout jumped in the streams as the mother and son panned for gold. Occasionally, hawks dove into the water close by and mule deer watched coyly from the woods beyond.

Abby emerged from the teepee attired in a dress with petticoats. She gathered up the beaver pelts.

"You must be going down to the Post," Blaine remarked.

His mother appeared uncomfortable as she climbed into the saddle, Winchester in tow. "I feel awkward in a skirt now that I'm accustomed to britches. But I don't want to end up arrested either. It's illegal for a woman to attire herself as a man and vice versa, you know."

Several days later she returned, waving a letter joyously in the air. "Charles sold our property in Gideon!" she shouted. He's opened a bank account for us in Ft. Morgan. I wrote and told him to take half and save it for Lorella."

"Half!" Blaine protested, "She's only entitled to one third."

"Remember, son, your sister lives in town," Abby explained. "She'll need that money more than we do."

"That's just an excuse! She doesn't deserve it! Little pale-skinned Lorella has never suffered. I alone in this family carry the burden of Indian blood. Always Lorella was the sacred one in your eyes."

"Oh, put a slug in it, Blaine! I'm weary of listening to you whine about all the ordeals and hardships due to your Indian blood. It's a chewed-out piece of tobacco."

"It's truth! All those times you let Jovah beat me, you did nothing! Yet the first time he went after Lorella you shot him dead!"

"She was only an infant, Blaine. Jovah would have killed her. You know it! Besides, the way you pummeled and mistreated Lorella every time my back was turned, I cringed every time I had to leave you alone together."

"She was part of Jovah! I could never forget that!"

"Well, it's damn fortunate for you I was able to lay my past experiences aside. Your Apache father was far more cruel and brutal," Abby told him. "Jovah was kind by comparison."

"You say that as if you did me a favor. I revile the moment you gave birth to me!" he shouted.

For the next several nights, the horrors of Abby's past returned in vivid nightmares to haunt her.

By late fall, a severe chill remained between mother and son. Snow had fallen and the frigid cold had already settled.

"We follow the stream and move further down the mountain," Abby told Blaine. "If we remain, we're liable to end up buried under snow. Besides, I plan to keep on the move. I've already alerted our kin in Ft. Morgan."

"Every time we get comfortable some place, we move," Blaine complained.

"It's part of life, son. Besides, I've a strange stirring, call it female intuition. I believe our true destiny is waiting beyond one of those mountains somewhere."

Several years pass.

# Chapter Eleven

Blaine did a double-take when his mother returned from a Trading Post with a pack-mule loaded with supplies. He almost dropped the axe as he chopped firewood.

"What is that hideous thing sticking out from your face?" he exclaimed.

Abby inhaled deeply on the cigar, before blowing a vapory ring of smoke. "I was wearing these britches as I came upon the new Post. Most of my hair was tucked under my jacket and my hat was down over my face. They mistook me for a man, and gave me a complimentary box of smokes. Now I've gone and acquired a taste for the damn things."

Blaine shook his head and chortled with amusement. "Well, don't fall asleep with one between your jaws and burn down the wigwam."

Abby dismounted the horse. She tugged on the waist of her britches. "Once I was proud of my slim contour," she recalled with a sigh.
"But way out here a body needs meat to survive, the kind marbled in fat. Well at least I'm still firm," she declared with pride.

"Physically, I'll bet you're as strong as any man your size," Blaine pointed out.

"We're trekking up the mountain tomorrow. We'll spend winter on the far side. We'll load the travois in the morning," she said.

The following day, the temperature remained below zero. However, there was no wind, so the journey was tolerable.

As they traveled, Blaine spotted a winding column of smoke rising atop the trees. "We're not alone."

"Let's head around the long way to where we can observe," Abby advised. "We don't want to walk straight into trouble."

Obscured by pine trees, they stood near the edge of a large clearing. Both fell silent in surprise. Before them lay a broad, two-story structure of felled logs. The lodge had a front and back porch, plus a small upstairs balcony.

"Who could possibly live in that, way up here?" Abby wondered aloud.

"Someone must. We saw the smoke," Blaine said.

"This may be a serious mistake, but I need to satisfy my curiosity." Abby cocked her rifle and proceeded forward.

Blaine quickly followed along with the Colt 45. He had grown nearly a foot taller than his mother.

The front door was unlatched. Abby and Blaine pushed it aside, and charged in. The large main room was empty.

"Someone is upstairs," Blaine whispered to his mother.

Abby heard the commotion, too. "We're armed! Come on down!" She hollered.

Several moments later, an Indian woman descended the staircase. She was pointing a Winchester of her own, and appeared on the verge of firing.

She was attired completely in fringed elk-skins; a handsome woman of indeterminate age; mature, but far from old.

"What are you doing here, squaw?" Abby snarled.

"Why do you invade my home?" the woman demanded to know. "Are you thieves?"

"No, we're just curious neighbors you might say. Lay your weapon down. We'll do likewise," Abby told her.

"Only a fool would be so trusting. As I recall, courteous neighbors first knock."

Blaine tossed his six-shooter to the floor. He encouraged a reluctant Abby to do the same. The Indian came down the steps into the main room. She was statuesque, her movements graceful.

Quickly she gathered up their firearms. "Who are you?" she asked suspiciously.

"I'm Abigail Cro...Colter, and this is my son Blaine."

"My birth-name is Whispering Wind," the Indian replied.

Before long she invited them to her table. Blaine and Abby were served a deliciously prepared meal of venison in a sumptuous, creamy sauce.

"It is a Gallic recipe," Whispering Wind said with a proud smile.

"So how did you end up alone, way out here?" Abby wanted to know.

"Some of my memories are painful to recall. Others are wondrous." She smiled wistfully. "I was born a Cheyenne. My village once lay in the hills just south of here. We existed peacefully, until story spread that our mountains possessed gold. A false rumor!" Her eyes narrowed bitterly. "At the time, the great war between the states waged in the east. The government desired any such gold to finance it."

"The blue-coated soldiers arrived with the first rays of dawn. Our teepees were set aflame and our livestock slaughtered, as were my people." Her jaw tightened. She paused to steady her anger. "My younger sister Starflower and I watched our family slain without pity."

"We escaped into the forest. We wandered for long weeks. Eventually, we had the misfortune of being captured by an Apache hunting party."

"I'm half Apache," Blaine interrupted.

Whispering Wind stared questioningly at Abby.

"It wasn't my choice," she replied matter-of-factly.

"The Apaches enslaved us," Whispering Wind continued. "We were treated harshly. My sister Starflower died of fever the first winter."

"Several years later, a Belgian aristocrat name Jules Van der Luis came through Indian territory with his entourage to hunt bison. He purchased me from the Apaches, for a lace tablecloth and a crystal decanter."

"Jules took me back to Europe with him. I lived as his mistress. To me, he seemed at first a deity. I was treated exquisitely. A tutor was hired to educate me. Jules even sent me to a finishing school in France. We journeyed extensively. For nearly twelve years, I led an exciting life of wonder and luxury."

"Jules assured me it would always remain such. Among other things, he promised me his hunting lodge in Scotland, a place where we shared many delightful memories. The majesty of the Scottish Highlands is unforgettable."

"Unfortunately, Jules was killed suddenly during a hunting jaunt. Being relatively young, his last will and testament was not yet revised. I was left destitute, his family unsympathetic to my plight."

"In desperation, I joined a circus in Paris. As an American Indian I was put on display in the freak show. I loathed it! I wore an outlandish costume of Spanish deerskin and Italian beads. Many patrons thought me a fraud. They accused me of being a Hindu, or even an Arab in disguise."

"After I had accumulated enough money, I boarded a ship bound for New York. I lived back east for several years. Because I speak fluent French, I acquired a top position in an exclusive restaurant. It was there that I met Noble." She closed her eyes as she smiled dreamily.

Abby was growing bored, while Blaine listened in fascination to each word.

"Noble became my husband. His father was a prominent architect, his mother an educated Cherokee. Noble was attending university at the time we met. He was a bit younger than I." She smiled rakishly.

"The plan was to follow his successful father's career. Noble was resigned to it, though he had limited interest in architecture.

"Eventually, however, to his parent's anguish, Noble left school and we were wed. I longed to return to the territory of my youth. The two of us built a small sheep ranch near the Wyoming border."

"We did not count upon the violent hostility of cattlemen. We were harassed and threatened constantly. Our sheep were all shot or poisoned. We were driven out.

"We came here. Noble and I built this lodge. Here, we lived freely as we chose, with no one to bother us."

"We're fugitives from society too," Blaine said. He proceeded to tell her of their own life's adventures.

"What happened to your man?" Abby asked the Indian woman.

"Sadly, our second winter here, Noble disappeared into a blizzard. Two days later, I found him, frozen to death." She paused to take a deep breath. "I buried him upon the mountaintop. This is my fourth winter without him. He was a brave spirit, and a noble man in every sense of the word. He is one with all creation now. I must not grieve."

"You and I have experienced much in common. Yet our experiences are quite different," Abby remarked. She looked the Indian woman up and down "You and I must be around the same age."

"It's regrettable our first encounter began as it did," Blaine said apologetically."

"You force me to confront my loneliness," Whispering Wind said. "Both of you may remain as long as you desire. I welcome your company."

Blaine was eager, but his mother was hesitant. At last, she relented. The lodge was certainly more spacious than a teepee. Each had a private bedroom upstairs. However, Abby felt uncomfortable with the arrangement.

Alone, inside her bedroom, she paused to study herself in the mirror. Abby was startled by the visage before her. She now understood why she never looked for very long at the reflection in mountain streams and lakes.

The long years of exposure to the elements had taken their toll. Her skin was leathery and deeply furrowed, and her hair had turned the color of dead leaves. Blaine often teased his mother that in certain light, her hair and skin appeared the same shade. Certainly the years had been far more benevolent to Whispering Wind.

"You are truly the most heroic person I have ever known," Blaine enthused to the Indian woman, as the three sat eating breakfast. "I am proud to know you. Your name sings off my tongue, Whispering Wind."

"Jules called me Winnie. It was a name given in affection. For that reason I kept it."

"We'll be on our way soon, Winnie," Abby announced.

Blaine looked over at his mother in startled surprise.

"But, you are welcome to remain and share my home," Whispering Wind reminded her.

"We must stay," Blaine beseeched. "We were meant to be here. I feel it inside."

Abby could not ignore the iron determination in her son's eyes.
"We'll linger awhile." She sighed. "But remember, this is not our home. Don't grow too content here."

Later, Abby watched Blaine coyly approach Whispering Wind. He seemed to believe his mother was out of earshot.

"Winnie, will you tell me of the Apaches? Always I've been curious. Mother refuses to speak of them."

Whispering Wind smiled fondly at Blaine. "It is your heritage. You have a right to this knowledge."

Blaine heaved a deep sigh of relief. Abby bit her lip.

"The Apache warrior possesses great cunning and strategy," she began. "Guile is ranked far above bravery. They call themselves warriors of the woods because winters are spent among the forests of the Sierra's. Above the plains, they observe all below. They are a tribe of perpetual wanderers, like gypsies." She smiled.

"And they thieve like gypsies, too!" Abby shouted. "Your memory is selective, Winnie. Explain to my son how torture is considered recreation. Give him a few examples. Shucks! The more horrid and lingering the victim's agony, the greater the Apaches revel in it, even their young'uns! Torture and thievery, that's what they live for!"

"Yes," Whispering Wind agreed. "Often the Apaches are indeed a cruel people. It arose out of the necessity to survive. However, they are no more savage than the white invaders, only without the hypocrisy. The greed and deceit of white men is unsurpassed."

“Please, I want to learn everything about my people.” Blaine persisted. He gazed searchingly at Whispering Wind.

“The Apaches consider all others beneath human,” Abby told him. “Enemies to them. Including the Cheyenne here.”

“Be proud of your heritage Blaine,” Whispering Wind said. “For there is much to take pride.”

“By God’s mercy, you were spared being raised an Apache. I’ll hear no more of this.” His mother was adamant.

“Please, Winnie, I must know,” Blaine continued to persist.

“Of course,” Whispering Wind said. “But some other time.”

Early the next day, to his mother’s annoyance, Blaine was again pestering their hostess for information. Patiently, Whispering Wind obliged him. Abby gnashed her teeth, while quietly eavesdropping.

“An Apache youth, such as yourself, is referred to as Ishkaynay. That remains until a trait of character distinguishes him, or perhaps even a noteworthy deed. Then he is bestowed his true name.”

“By right I should have an Apache name,” Blaine declared. “Please tell me more.”

“Well,” she paused to recall. “There is a great amount. But I know you will learn swiftly.”

She reached for a bow and arrow. “These are used for night attack. A far better weapon than the firearm to kill in silence; perfect for the hunt! Prey aplenty is brought down before most of the flock, or herd, takes flight or flees.”

“Will you teach me how to make a bow and arrow?” Blaine asked hopefully.

Whispering Wind nodded. “An Apache arrow has three feathers with an iron head. The materials exist all around us. First, I’ll show you how to string a bow.”

“Blaine,” his mother interrupted. “We’re growing short of supplies. It’s time you and I went searching for a Trading Post.”

“There is a Post four days from here, down the far side of the east mountain,” Whispering Wind told her. “It’s operated by an old woman named Mary Peppertree. She is fair and honorable.”

“Son, come along. You can help me locate it.”

“You’re up to finding it yourself,” Blaine curtly replied.

“The trail is marked by initials carved into the trees. N.T. for Noble Trulock,” Winnie said.

Abby sighed deeply. "I'll be back in eight days time. I can't depart this place fast enough," she murmured under her breath.

If it had been possible, Abby would have physically snatched up her son and permanently departed the territory.

Upon her return, she discovered Whispering Wind instructing Blaine how to wield a long, Indian lance. In the other hand, he carried a shield of triple-antelope hide ornamented with brass studs fashioned from buttons.

Abby was horrified by the sight. "Blaine! Drop that! Toss it away. Better yet, burn it! I was a fool to leave. I could have foreseen this. I knew this copper-skin bitch was a heinous influence."

"Blaine is entitled to learn." Whispering Wind stepped forward to confront her. "You would deprive your son his birthright?"

"Damn right I would! I'm his mama, not you! Whatever concerns my son, I decide!"

"No!" protested Blaine. "No longer am I a child. It is I who will decide."

Abby could see argument was useless. Seething, she proceeded to unload the supplies alone. She watched and listened as Whispering Wind continued to instruct her son in the ways of a warrior.

"I have a gift for you," Whispering Wind said to Blaine. She disappeared briefly into the lodge. Several moments later, she emerged with a scarlet silk scarf. "This was given to me in Paris." She smiled. "This color is greatly admired by Apaches." She tied it to his lance as a pennon.

Blaine appeared exultant, as Abby fumed inside.

"I have a gift for you too, son, from the Post," she told him later that evening. Abby presented him with a fresh razor. "Those dark bristles on your handsome jaw grow back way too fast."

"Curse my white blood," he replied. "It shames me,"

"You've inherited your Grandpa Henry's thick whiskers, also his tolerance."

By the end of the summer, Blaine possessed a quiver filled with arrows. He had already become as skilled a hunter with a bow, as he was a marksman with a six-gun.

"I have a name for you now," Whispering Wind announced. "Henceforth, you shall be known as Nahkahyen. It means keen-sighted to the Apaches."

Pleased and proud, Blaine repeated the name over and over again to himself. His mother was extremely unnerved.

It was growing difficult to distinguish where Blaine's admiration of Whispering Wind ended, and his adoration began.

Abby was forced to make another sojourn to the Trading Post for more supplies. Upon her return, she was silent, but visibly upset. A letter was flung across the table.

“”Eudora and Charles want to adopt Lorella,” she said.

“So?” Blaine shrugged.

“So you and I are heading to Ft. Morgan! We're bringing Lorella back with us. I ain't giving up my child.”

“You already did. It's too late.” Blaine pointed out. “Lorella doesn't belong here.”

“You don't understand, son. They want me to sign papers, to give up all legal claim to her, as though I won't be her mama anymore.”

“Well, I think it's a fine idea.”

“Pack up! We're leaving at dawn.”

“No, I'll remain. It doesn't concern me.”

“Lorella is your sister,” Abby reminded him.

“She belongs where she is. Lorella isn't like us. She's like all those others. I'm staying.” Blaine glared at his mother unflinchingly.

“All right, stay here and play games with Winnie, be a pretend Apache. But I'm keeping my kin together. The time has come to get Lorella.”

Abby departed as the first rays of sunlight emerged through the thick mountain trees. She glanced back at the lodge for a final look. A sudden chilling sensation shot through her. Abby shook it off, and continued on her way.

# Chapter Twelve

Ft. Morgan had grown so rapidly it first appeared a different town. Plus the O'Briens had moved to a new address, one unfamiliar to Abby.

People were staring. Suddenly aware of her surroundings, Abby pulled the cigar from her lips, and crushed it beneath the heel of her high-laced shoe. These shoes, and the dress she wore felt strange and uncomfortable now.

The new O'Brien home was lavish with spacious bay windows, towers, and balconies. With mixed feelings, Abby knocked on the door.

A maid answered, and summoned Charles. He was much heavier and grayer. He greeted Abby, but did not appear to recognize her, until she spoke. He appeared dismayed at the sight of her.

Abby complimented him upon the house.

"My emporium has proved more successful than I ever dared to hope." He beamed proudly. "Come wait in the parlor. Mae is out shopping with Eudie."

"Who?" Abby was puzzled.

"Uh, Lorella prefers her middle moniker. Everyone in Ft. Morgan knows her as Mae O'Brien."

"Oh, you take a lot for granted, don't you?"

"It was Mae's choice. Eudora and I respect her wishes. We've noticed from your letters, you're back to using your maiden name."

"I keep trying to bury my past." Abby sighed wearily. "But it always seems to resurrect itself to haunt me."

At that moment, convivial, laughing voices were heard from an adjoining room. Charles called out to them.

Eudora entered the parlor first. She seemed so tiny and frail now. However, her eyes remained merry and full of fire. Carefully, she looked Abby up and down.

"Mae!" she hollered. "Come in and greet your mother. She's twelve years old now," Eudora told Abby.

"Thirteen, the end of next month," the girl added, as she boldly sashayed into the room. Lorella was attired in chic satin and lace. She stared at her mother as if a stranger.

The girl appeared closer to fifteen, Abby thought. Her greetings caught in her throat. Abby rushed to embrace her daughter. Lorella seemed restrained, almost cold.

"You look so different," she remarked to her mother.

"And so do you! Time leaves nothing unchanged. Let me have another look. By the way, Blaine sends his love. He misses you, too."

A grim expression swept over the girl's face.

"He's sorry he couldn't come," Abby continued," but he had other matters to attend. We're living in a big lodge high in the mountains. It's magnificent up there. Wouldn't you love to see it?"

"About the matter at hand," Mrs. O'Brien interjected. "We already regard Mae as our child. The legal documents shall make it official."

"Eudora, please," Charles admonished. "There's plenty of time for this, not now."

"I won't wait," his wife declared. "I love Mae as my own. If you truly care for her welfare, Abby, you'll sign."

"Certainly she will," the child stated matter-of-factly. "My mother would want me to be happy."

"Yes, Lorella." Abby smiled. "I want you to come back with me. I'll make you happy, I promise."

The look displayed upon the girl's face startled and saddened her mother.

"I've come to take you home. We've missed you dearly."

"This is my home!" she screamed. "I don't want to live in an old mountain lodge like some tomfool simpleton."

"Lorella please, hear me out."

"My name is Mae! If you force me, I'll hate you!"

Dejected, Abby watched as her daughter stormed from the parlor in tears. Abby's shoulders drooped, she sighed in resignation. "Bring me the papers. I'll sign."

Afterward, she announced she would be leaving the following day. Charles and Eudora protested, insisting she remain for a visit, and reacquaint herself with her child.

"No." She shrugged. "It's for Lorella's peace of mind that I leave."

"I'll go tell Mae," Eudora volunteered.

"I brought an extra horse. Didn't expect to be going back alone," Abby told Charles. "I've just lost a child. And worse, it's exactly what Lorella desired." She wept.

"I've something to make you feel better, at least for awhile." He smiled sympathetically as he reached for a decanter. He proceeded to pour her a shot of whiskey. "This will numb your pain."

At first Abby refused. "All those years in the saloon, and later married to Jovah and I never took a drink."

Reluctantly, she held the glass to her lips. She didn't like the taste. But after awhile, even that improved. The following morning, she was too sick to travel.

Charles felt guilty and responsible. Eudora was disgusted. Abby was ashamed before her daughter, who refused to converse with her.

The next morning Abby arose in darkness, long before the household had arisen. She departed quietly leaving behind sealed notes, one addressed to Lorella, the other to the O'Briens.

Upon her journey home, Abby picked up several bottles of whiskey at Trading Posts along the way. "I've lost her," she repeated to herself in whispers.

At last Abby came upon familiar terrain. As she followed the stream up the mountain, she heard robust laughter in the distance. Abby dismounted her horse, and stealthily crept through the brush for a better look.

A nude Blaine and Whispering Wind were playfully splashing and bathing each other in the stream. Abby continued to watch in anguished silence. To her shock and dismay the two tightly embraced before kissing feverishly, and disappearing momentarily beneath the rippling waters. They re-emerged still clinging to each other and laughing heartily.

Abby possessed no desire to see more. Abruptly, she returned to the horses and proceeded to the lodge.

Several hours seemed to pass before Blaine and Whispering Wind returned. Their mirthful laughter preceded them as they joyously charged, stark naked into the room. Their expressions froze upon their faces. Whispering Wind stepped behind Blaine to cover herself. She draped her arms around him.

"Mama!" Blaine exclaimed. "We didn't expect to see you for at least another week."

"I saw what you two have been doing while I was gone. Shame on you! Especially you, Winnie. But then I forgot, you prefer young boys green off the vine. Pack-up, Blaine. We're clearing out of here!"

"No, you go!" Blaine shouted. "My place is here, beside Whispering Wind. I love her!"

"You're talking like an ass! Your lust for the old squaw is addling your reasoning."

"Your son and I intend to wed. We wish for you to remain," Whispering Wind said as she glanced nervously at Blaine. "We want your blessing."

"You're the cause of our misery, you copper-skinned whore! I'm taking my son and leaving."

"You leave, I'm staying!" Blaine shouted.

"You think Blaine a boy, but he is a man," Whispering Wind said.

"And you, with those Apache lessons and games. You're turning my son into exactly what I tried to prevent him from becoming," Abby snarled.

"I gave Blaine pride. You gave him shame he did nothing to deserve." She stepped forward forgetting her nakedness.

With that, Abby struck the Indian woman so forcefully Whispering Wind bounced from the wall before landing on the wood floor. As she rolled on her side, Winnie pulled down a hunting knife hanging from a wall hook. Crouching, she aimed it menacingly at Abby. Blaine quickly stepped between them

"If you attack me again, you'll carry my mark across your face for life," the Indian woman threatened.

"The Apaches should have held onto you." Abby sniffed.

Blaine helped Whispering Wind to her feet.

"I want to speak to my son alone. Vamoose!"

"Winnie, stay!" Blaine demanded.

"No." She shook her head. "I'm going upstairs. But don't forget, this is my home, and you are a guest," she told Abby.

The two of them watched her leave.

"Well I'm damn glad your little sister didn't return with me now. Lorella'd be plenty embarrassed by your bawdy behavior, the way you two were carrying on like a couple of rutting animals in the wild."

"I knew Lorella would never come," Blaine stated matter-of-factly. "She's ashamed of us both."

The words shook Abby. She walked over to a backpack strewn across a chair, and produced a bottle of whiskey.

Blaine appeared startled. "When did you start drinking that stuff?"

"I bought it to comfort me, and keep me warm when winter comes."

"So, I was right about Lorella, wasn't I?"

"You could say that. Lorella is now going by the name of Mae O'Brien."

Blaine forced a bitter laugh. At the same time he appeared to gloat. The discussion of his paramour was apparently over, for now.

The tension in the lodge soon became almost unbearable to Abby. She and Whispering Wind seldom spoke now. Blaine had become increasingly defiant and quarrelsome. Also, there were the furtive glances, secret whispers, and sly, knowing smiles between her son and Winnie, and the sighs and moans in the night.

Summer slowly cooled into Fall. Abby was returning from the Trading Post. Whispering Wind had prepared a delicacy.

"Your son killed this mountain lion with his bow and arrow this morning." She glanced proudly at Blaine.

Abby looked down at the table and grimaced. "You mean we're now eating like Apaches, too. I ate mountain lion once. Never again."

"But you've never tasted it with my Parisian herb sauce."

"I'll forgo the pleasure." Abby headed for the cabinet drawer. She pulled out a bottle of whiskey and went out to the front porch.

Later Blaine joined her. "Why must you constantly insult Winnie?" he demanded to know.

"My instincts warned me that squaw was poison from our first encounter."

"Winnie and I plan to wed in the Spring, the most beautiful and sacred of all seasons."

"She's too old for you, son. You're being unwise." Abby tried to stand, but staggered.

Blaine caught her, and helped her regain her balance.

"You're becoming a drunken sot, just like Jovah. I hate it!"

"You forget son, we enjoyed good times with Jovah, too."

"Those times did not outweigh the tears and the anguish. Did you forget?" Blaine gnashed his teeth.

"Do you want to know about your father, Chief Raging Storm? He was cruel and violent, and he commanded no respect from me. He beat me with far more zeal than Jovah ever did. And starved me, too."

"Also I was forced to endure brutal abuse and debasement from his other squaws. So pardon me if I have no desire to have Apache tradition thrown in my face like cow dung." Abby took another long chug of whiskey.

Soon the freezing winds of winter swept in and the temperature dropped below zero. The snow drifts were so deep sometimes they could only leave the lodge through its upstairs balcony.

One afternoon, Abby and Blaine were outside hunting, but not for long. Soon they fled back to the lodge avoiding a ravenous wolf pack on their heels. Whispering Wind helped them to shove furniture up against doors and windows. The hungry pack snarled and howled just outside.

"They have tasted human flesh. I can tell," Whispering Wind said.

The following day Abby and Blaine set out hunting again in the drifting snow. Before long the two had wandered apart.

The freezing, icy winds kicked up and began to howl. Or was it the wolves? Abby wondered. In no time, she found herself in the middle of a blinding blizzard. Through determination, she found her way back to the lodge.

"Where is Blaine?" Whispering Wind asked with alarm.

Abby heaved and caught her breath before she spoke. "I had hoped he made it back before me."

The Indian woman bundled herself in heavy clothes and furs. She grabbed up her Winchester. "I'm going to find him," she said.

"Blaine will find his way back," Abby assured her.

"You don't understand. I lost Noble to a blizzard. I won't sit here waiting and allow it to occur all over again."

"We're both fools, but I'm going too," Abby told her.

The two women were quickly separated as they trudged blindly through the icy, howling storm in opposite directions. Both were screaming Blaine's name.

Abby heard a faint third voice. The howling winds grew louder, and more bone-chilling. Blaine was calling out to her. Abby followed the sound of his voice. The howling resounded throughout the brittle, freezing air. Only it wasn't the wind, it was the wolves.

In horror, Abby shrieked out her son's name.

Nightmarish piercing screeches, snarls, and growls resonated through the icy air along with shrill wails, followed by rapid blasts of gunfire.

Prepared for death, Abby hastened toward the ghastly sounds, her rifle cocked, and ready to fire. They led her to Blaine, who almost shot her, mistaking his mother for a wolf.

"No, Blaine! It's me!" she screamed.

"They got Winnie!" he cried. Tears had already frozen on his face in icicles.

"Come, we've got to make it back to the lodge, son."

"No!" Blaine shrieked, "I must hunt them down and slaughter them all! Winnie! Winnie!"

"That won't help her now. We must escape ourselves. Else we'll freeze to death, and those four-legged hell hounds will be feasting on our carcasses too."

Steering blindly through the blowing snow and ice, Abby led a grieving, near-hysterical Blaine back safely to the lodge.

"Winnie is gone," Blaine repeated over and over in disbelief.

By mid afternoon of the following day, the storm had attenuated. Blaine raced out upon the snow, searching everywhere. Abby followed along, a distance behind.

"Winnie." Blaine choked as he wept. "We must give her a sacred Indian burial," he announced.

"Look around son. There aren't enough of her remains to bury."

"Then I'll bury all her possessions, up there, upon this mountaintop, next to Noble. Apaches refuse to keep possessions of their dead loved ones. It's asking for misfortune."

"But she was Cheyenne, son."

Blaine ignored his mother. He hurried back to the lodge. Busily he gathered up bundle after bundle of Whispering Wind's belongings. Then he built a horse travois to carry them up the mountain.

"That grave is going to be enormous enough for ten people," Abby remarked. "You may as well dig her a pit."

Blaine suddenly realized his mother made sense. "Perhaps just her most treasured items." He began unloading the travois. Soon Blaine started up the mountain.

"Wait!" Abby hollered. "It'll be dark soon. At least wait till morning."

"Apache burials take place at night," he informed her.

"You're burying a Cheyenne," Abby reminded him once again. "Are you doing this for Whispering Wind or yourself? Winnie was only a captive, like me. She probably hated the Apaches."

"At least Winnie laid her hatred aside for me."

"Dig that grave deep, son. Then jump in yourself! That squaw owns you now."

Later during the wee, pitch black hours after midnight, Abby heard Indian chanting echoing down from the mountaintop. It haunted her dreams. Blasts of gunfire were heard in the distance. After nearly a week, Blaine returned.

His skin was drawn and tired-looking; his eyes vacant and swollen from grieving. He appeared older.

"I slaughtered those wolves," Blaine said. "Now we must leave here; leave Winnie's lodge forever."

"What?" Abby asked in disbelief. "Why?"

"I told you before. Apaches consider it damn bad luck to use any possessions of their dead. We'll burn this place before we leave."

"Well, I'm no Apache, thank goodness, and neither was your old squaw. This is our lodge now. Besides, finally there's a tranquil air to this place." Abby smiled broadly, her eyes closed in satisfaction.

"You're actually pleased that Winnie is dead. I hate you so much this moment!" shouted Blaine.

Abby could not deny it. Secretly and often, she had wished the Indian woman dead. And worse, she felt no guilt for those thoughts, not even now.

Blaine immediately moved out. He set up a teepee by the stream, but within sight of the lodge. He attired himself wholly in buckskins, well tanned, as Whispering Wind had instructed, and plain as the Apaches prefer. He began to let his hair grow long. Already it swept his shoulders. Blaine seemed to take delight in his mother's stares of disapproval. He strutted proudly before her.

Later Abby found a pair of sheep shears in the back of a drawer.

"These should do it," she whispered to herself.

Several hours later, Blaine returned from checking his traps. He was shocked and dumbfounded as he first spied his mother. Her hair had been sheared dramatically short. He raced to her side for a closer look.

"You, you look exactly like a man!" he exclaimed.

"I should have done this ages ago. Long hair is too much bother out here. You'll find out. Ironic, isn't it?"

"I can never go back to what I was. I'm different now," Blaine announced with pride.

"Winnie turned you into exactly what I was determined to prevent you from becoming," Abby lamented.

"You couldn't even save yourself, Ma."

The alienation between them festered and grew as the years passed.

# Chapter Thirteen

Abby returned late one day from the Trading Post. Her leathery complexion appeared a mass of deep trenches in the glaring winter sunlight. Blaine now had long braids reaching below his chest. He watched his mother ride up the path.

"Old Mary Peppertree is dead. Age finally brought her down," Abby lamented. "Mary's nephew, Jarvis Rutmore runs the place now. Poor fool honestly believes me to be a man."

"That grating voice of yours has gotten awful husky and deep from tobacco and whiskey. And you certainly appear the part." He looked at her with disdain. "Did Mary's nephew swoon when he learned the truth?"

"I didn't bother to straighten him out," Abby replied. "Men only talk down to women. It gives them a false superiority. I'm tired of dealing with that nonsense. He only knows me as Colter. Fortunately all the other regulars have drifted away."

Abby pulled a letter from her jacket. "My persistence wasn't in vain. Lorella has finally answered my mail."

"Lorella!" Blaine exclaimed. "She disowned us years ago! Look at all your letters she ignored. She wouldn't even write after Aunt Eudie died. Lorella must want something."

"Charles re-married too quickly after Eudora's passing." Abby sighed. "That Lydia woman knew he and Mae were not blood-kin. She felt uncomfortable with her around, Lorella says. Charles never mentioned any of this in his letters."

"And I'll just wager she hadn't a clue Miss Mae possessed Indian blood for that matter." Blaine snorted.

"Lorella's working now as a governess to the Strickland family in Denver. Also she's engaged to be married, next Christmas. Her fiancé's name is Ruben, she says."

"Christmas!" Blaine exclaimed. "That's nearly a year. He'll be wise to her kind by then."

"I'm sure they have their reasons for waiting," his mother told him. "Besides, this will give us plenty of time. Lorella's our close kin. We should see her, to wish her well, before she's wed and begins a new life."

“Lorella may as well be dead to me. And you, too. Remember, she’s Miss Mae O’Brien now.”

“Blaine, you should be ashamed. She’s our blood! We’re both going. I insist! You have an obligation to your sister.”

“Half-sister,” he corrected with a sneer. “I’ve severed all ties, you understand?”

Abby shot him a scowl. However, she was determined to create peace in the family before she became old and passed on. Besides, she longed to see Lorella again.

Determined, Abby pleaded, badgered, and cajoled Blaine at every opportunity. Eventually, to silence her, he reluctantly agreed; else that or shoot her, he reasoned.

“Only this once. Never again.” He was adamant.

By May the weather had warmed enough for the journey. In Denver, Abby spied a dress hanging on a rack as she peered through a shop window. Inside, she also purchased a ruffled bonnet decorated with flowers. Later she bought some light-toned face powder and rouge.

“I don’t want Lorella thinking her mama has changed into a man.” She giggled to a scowling Blaine.

“You look like an old Madam, but not quite as good,” he commented upon first seeing her in costume.

“I never used powder or rouge as a girl. Back then I didn’t need it.” She sighed wistfully.

Abby insisted he discard his buckskins for the visit. She tied Blaine’s long hair into a single tight braid. She then tucked it down inside his shirt, under his jacket, concealing it beneath the collar. A broad-brimmed hat was added to complete the attire.

“I still look like an Indian. Only in white man’s clothes,” he seethed.

“At least you don’t look like some illiterate savage.” She gazed him up and down. “In fact you’re right handsome, son. The Strickland’s are a prominent Denver family.”

Blaine cringed. “They must live in the same area as Meredith Birkshire. That old bitch forbade us to return to Denver, remember?”

Abby laughed. “Old Meredith has been getting her privates groped by demons in hell for ages now, according to Lorella.”

“So, does Miss Mae know we’re arrived for a visit?” Blaine sniffed.

“Why certainly. Lorella has set aside this evening. I’m renting a buggy for the occasion. We’re expected around seven.”

Abby, posture perfect as always, rode in the buggy. Blaine followed behind on horseback. Several blocks from the Strickland house, one of the buggy horses went lame. Blaine jumped from his mount.

"There's a stable a'ways back. I'll go fetch a fresh horse," he volunteered.

"No, I'll tend to it, son. I'm not one of those helpless, dainty dolls you see strutting the boulevards. According to the address, the Strickland estate must be that gigantic house with columns at the end of the street. Lorella is waiting. You go on ahead and explain what happened."

"Me! Why? You should go, Ma."

"The good Lord caused this to happen for a reason, son. This is the chance for you and Lorella to make peace between yourselves alone."

Grumbling and cursing beneath his breath, Blaine approached the Strickland mansion. Never would he do his mother another favor, he vowed. Night was falling and the air was growing cold.

Nervously, he prepared to knock. Instead, Blaine walked over and peered through the window. The spacious room seemed almost incandescent; the oil lamps burned, candelabra's flickered, and the fireplace blazed.

A slim, graceful, extremely attractive young woman stepped into view. Lorella? Blaine was uncertain.

She gazed over toward the window. From her expression, Blaine knew she could only see his movements outside the glass. He tapped on the pane.

She departed the room, as Blaine hurried over to the door. Upon opening it, she gasped at the sight of him.

"Lorella? Lorella, is that you?"

"Mae," she corrected. "I assumed you were aware of that." She beckoned him inside, into the incandescent parlor.

Her beauty was striking. Lustrous black tresses highlighted her eyes; eyes bluer than turquoise, softer than flowers, as Jovah used to say of Abby.

Blaine explained their mother's delay. "Where are the Stricklands?" he was curious to know.

"The family is visiting relations."

"Ma said you were insistent we come this particular evening. Now it's clear why. You didn't want your kin embarrassing you in front of the uppity rich folk. Right, Lorella?"

"Can you fault me for it? I never felt a true sense of bliss or peace- of-mind until I distanced myself from you!" She almost spat the words into his face. Her eyes were intense, unblinking.

Blaine seethed with anger. As he was about to verbally assail his sister, a loud knocking interrupted his thoughts.

"That must be Ma." Lorella hastened from the room.

Blaine heard a man's voice bellow out a greeting.

"Ruben, I told you I wasn't up to seeing you this evening." His sister sounded agitated.

"But Mae, now that you're all alone here, we can use the time to our pleasure."

"Ruben please, not this particular evening. Go away."

"Oh? Are you entertaining another suitor behind my back? Is there another man here?" He chuckled.

Blaine heard his footsteps coming toward the room.

As he stepped inside the brightly lit parlor, Ruben froze abruptly upon spotting Blaine standing by the fireplace. His convivial manner evaporated. "Who is this?  Mae, who is this man?"

Lorella became visibly shaken. She stumbled uncomfortably for an answer.

"Mae, what's wrong? What are you doing with someone like this?" Her fiancé looked Blaine over condescendingly. "Who are you? Did he force his way in here, dear Mae?"

"No, no, it's all right." She swallowed deeply. "Please Ruben, I'll explain later."

"I'm her brother," Blaine boldly announced.

Ruben glared at his fiancé in disbelief. "But, but this man is a half-breed, Mae."

"He is only my half-brother," she explained.

"You speak as if you possessed no Indian blood yourself," Blaine said.

"What?" Ruben exclaimed with astonishment.

"Her true name is Lorella Mae True-Crows, not Mae O'Brien. Her papa was a half-breed like me."

"Blaine, please!" Lorella bristled.

"I see you're not denying this, Mae," Ruben sadly remarked.

"It had no bearing on our relationship. Do you love me any less? I was planning to tell you, my darling, I swear. I only needed the right moment."

"When? Perhaps on our 50th wedding anniversary! You deceived me, Mae. That is what I never will forgive!" He pushed her roughly out of his way as he stormed from the parlor.

"Ruben, try to understand. Please wait!"

However, her cries were ignored. Coldly, Lorella turned to confront her brother.

"You must hate me to the depths of your soul. What did I ever do to you? Damn you, Blaine!"

Outside, Abby pulled up in the buggy just as Ruben was leaving. She watched him intently with curiosity. Ruben did not appear to even notice her. Distraught and preoccupied, he mounted a beautiful thoroughbred, and quickly galloped away down the opposite side of the boulevard.

Lorella was inconsolable. The presence of her mother and Blaine only seemed to upset her more. Their visit was brief. Abby was infuriated with Blaine.

"Why can't you allow any of us to be happy?" she hollered. "Why must you deliberately ruin everything?"

"I didn't expect that pompous dandy of a fiancé to show and look down on me like filth. Besides, I never wanted to come to Denver. You insisted! That was a mistake!"

"Nothing is ever your fault, is it son?" Abby grimaced. "We'll leave tomorrow. I'll send an apology to Lorella. After what happened, I'm ashamed to face her again. I wouldn't blame her if she disowned us now."

"She did that years ago, Ma."

"Well, ain't it a wonder!" Abby's countenance hardened like a rock as she glowered at Blaine. "I just hope that Ruben truly loves her. If so, he'll forgive her and come back."

Blaine snorted and rolled his eyes at those words.

The following day, they began the arduous journey home. Both were anxious to leave Denver. Also they were relieved to discard the uncomfortable city clothes.

Three-quarters of the way, they camped for the night beside a mountain creek. Blaine swore he heard a mournful sobbing in the wind. Abby dismissed it as his imagination.

The following night as they camped in the forest, Blaine insisted they were being followed. He placed his ear to the ground.

"Now I'm certain," he proclaimed.

Abby quickly put out the fire. "We'll separate. Circle around that way," she whispered. "Someone may be out to rob us."

The two mounted up. Abby watched Blaine disappear through the darkness of the dense woods. As she rode through the moonless night, Abby listened to the hoof-beats of a strange horse coming from the opposite direction.

Stealthily, she paused in hiding, waiting for the unknown rider to pass. A dark cloak and hood could be seen flapping in the wind, upon a horse as black as the night itself.

Without warning, Blaine suddenly darted before the startled rider; his six-gun drawn and cocked. A woman's scream pierced the chilly night air. Abby emerged from the dense foliage.

"Who are you?" Abby demanded, as she galloped closer.

"Get away! Don't touch me!" the woman hollered. She kicked her heels deeply into the horse, attempting to flee.

Blaine adroitly seized the reins. The woman's screams resounded through the forest.

"Shut up! We're not going to harm you!" Abby shrieked. She jerked the hood from the woman's head. "Lorella!"

Abby and Blaine leaned closer. The young woman's demeanor showed confusion. She glanced back and forth at the two in puzzlement.

"Lorella, you followed us, why?" Abby wanted to know.

"Mama? Blaine?" she asked in dire amazement. "I thought, I mean, you…you look exactly like a man." She then gazed at her brother. "Blaine's hair is so long suddenly. And why is he all dressed in buckskins, like…"

"Like a savage?" Blaine snapped.

Abby shot him a baleful glance. "You might say we were in costume, back in Denver," she told Lorella. "This is our customary attire."

Lorella appeared incredulous. Abby and Blaine led her back to their campsite where Blaine rebuilt the campfire.

"So what's wrong?" Abby asked her daughter. "It has to do with our visit, doesn't it?"

Lorella glowered malevolently at Blaine, she nodded.

"Appears I've been driven out of Denver twice in one lifetime. Vanessa, Ruben's mother banished me. Also the Strickland's dismissed me without explanation."

Abby gazed at Blaine, her eyes shooting hellfire.

"Vanessa was absolutely wonderful to me in the beginning," Lorella continued. "She gave me a solid gold heirloom locket with Ruben's portrait inside. The last time I saw her she ripped it from my throat." Lorella choked back tears.

Abby threw her arms around the girl. She stroked Lorella's long, ebony curls. "Folks are seldom as fine and decent as they pretend to be," she told her. "What about that Ruben? Wasn't he man enough to stand up to his mama?"

Sadly, Lorella shook her head. "I'm carrying his child. I told Vanessa of the baby and she called me a whore! Ruben is now denying the child is his. He claimed we never even...How could he forsake me?" She sobbed. "And worse, everyone has taken his side and branded me. I'm socially ruined. It doesn't matter that I'm Charles O'Brien's stepdaughter."

"They must be wealthy folk I take it," said Abby. "Wealthy, pretentious hypocrites, I know their ilk well."

"I swear to God, it was Ruben I loved, not his wealth," Lorella insisted. "Before your visit we were planning to elope, early next month at the latest. We couldn't wait for a Christmas wedding."

"Obviously," Blaine said dryly.

Abby gritted her teeth. Lorella broke into wailing sobs.

"I would have been honored to be Mrs. Ruben Jefferson Osbourne, even if the world collapsed tomorrow and everything was lost!" she cried.

"Osbourne?" Osbourne, the name struck a raw nerve inside of Abby. "Is his papa named Alexander Osbourne? Lorella don't lie to me."

The girl appeared distraught and nervous; she began to tremble. "I hoped you'd forget. That all happened so long ago."

The wrath Abby felt for Blaine was now directed toward Lorella. "Some things are seared so deeply into your soul, the ache and torment is forever. You certainly should understand this!"

"I do now, Mama."

"That Vanessa bitch must be Jess Atkinhead's sister and your precious Ruben his nephew. That explains plenty! You know the character of these people, Lorella! You should have expected as much or worse."

"But none of the past was Ruben's fault. He could be so genuinely warm and thoughtful."

"Yeah, at first they all are," Abby told her. "Does the illustrious Osbourne family remember us?"

"I don't think so. Ruben didn't make the connection, thank God."

"You're with us now. Everything will be all right," Abby assured her. "I'll solve your little problem before it grows too big."

Abby and Blaine took Lorella back to their secluded mountain retreat. Abby pointed to the lodge.

"I inherited this place from the previous owner, a squaw named Winnie Trulock," she told her.

Blaine narrowed his eyes at his mother as they dismounted. His jaw tightened.

Abby seized Lorella by the hand. "How far along are you, dear?"

"Ah, not very, perhaps a month."

Abby nodded in satisfaction. "That makes it all the easier. I'll dig out a darning needle in the morning."

"What for?"

Lorella and Blaine stared at her in dismay. Abby only smiled knowingly.

"You're going to kill my baby!" Lorella exclaimed.

"You bet! And I might even mail it all fancied-up in colored paper and ribbons to your Ruben as an early Christmas present."

Lorella was horrified, Blaine was incredulous.

"Never! This child is all I've left of Ruben," lamented Lorella.

"You surprise me, Ma," Blaine said. "You always told me you reviled that practice at the saloon."

"I won't allow a bastard child to ruin the rest of Lorella's life." Abby bristled.

"You mean the way I ruined yours?" he replied.

Abby winced. She led Lorella into the lodge. Blaine withdrew to his teepee.

Several hours later, Abby found Lorella seated by a back window, sobbing.

"You'd be foolish to birth this young'un," Abby told her. "I speak from experience. Do you want a constant reminder of your humiliation? Ruben never loved you! That should be clear now. He only wanted you as a possession. The way Jess wanted me. You bear this child and you'll live with that mistake for an entire lifetime. Think, Lorella!"

"I don't know, Ma. It seems unnatural somehow."

"Lorella, if you possessed an ounce of good judgment, you wouldn't have taken up with Jess Atkinhead's nephew."

Lorella grimaced, arose and quickly walked away. She disappeared into another room, locking it behind her.

Abby went to Winnie's old room. She sifted through her things searching for a darning needle. Eventually she found a couple in the back of the closet.

"Are you certain you possess the skill to do this?" Blaine later asked her.

"The procedure isn't that difficult," Abby replied. "I watched Sadie do it dozens of times."

"But that was ages ago, Ma."

"My hands are as steady as ever, Blaine."

Early the following morning, Abby carefully sterilized one of the needles inside the hearth's fire. She called out Lorella's name. No answer was forthcoming.

Abby ran upstairs. A few seconds later she hurried to Blaine's teepee. "Lorella's gone!" she cried. "Her valise, too! Damn her! Mount up. Help me fetch her back."

Blaine shook his head and sat down. "She's made her decision, Ma, let her go."

Exasperated, Abby wandered the mountainside on horseback calling out Lorella's name.

Later in the day, she came across Blaine as he was hunting deer in the far valley.

"Lorella's too far ahead!" he shouted. "Go back to your lodge."

"She's acting like a fool. Only she won't realize it until too late," Abby lamented.

Several days passed, Abby was outside checking traps. Angry, strident voices carried through the wind. She followed the sound.

A weary and disheveled-looking Lorella stood by the mountain stream with Blaine. They were quarrelling fervidly and bitterly. Abby heard Lorella using language uncustomary for a proper young lady.

"Lorella!" she exclaimed. "You've returned. You've changed your mind!"

"No," the girl replied. "I got lost. I'm unfamiliar with the terrain."

"Lorella was saying she was afraid she might spawn a scourged bastard like me." Blaine fumed. "She doesn't want a bad-luck seed."

"You won't have to," Abby assured her. "Why you must be half-starved, Lorella. Come; let's head back to the lodge."

Abby prepared a generous serving of venison stew. As the young girl quickly gulped her food, Abby went upstairs to find the darning needle.

As she was bringing it down, Abby concealed it behind her back. She watched Lorella push the empty bowl away. Abby slipped the needle inside her jacket. She approached her daughter.

"Truly, you don't want to bear that child, Lorella. You can't!"

"To be honest, Mama, I do and I don't."

"But that young'un, it carries Jess Atkinhead's blood."

"That's really why you want to destroy it, isn't it?"

"Don't you recall what he did to me? And he almost burned the three of us alive!"

"I certainly fared little better with the Osbournes." Lorella sighed.

"We can't wait forever to do this, Lorella."

"I don't know. It still feels wrong somehow."

"Please trust me, Lorella."

"It seems unnatural. I'm scared, Mama."

"I asked you to trust me, Lorella. I'm your mama; I'd never do anything to harm you. I'd take a 45 slug through the heart to protect you."

The girl forced a wan smile. She reached for her mother's hand, squeezing the fingers tightly.

Abby was eager to perform the procedure before Lorella changed her mind. She heated the needle in the hearth's fire.

Lorella began to cry. "Mama, I can't do this."

"Trust me, Lorella," she whispered to the young girl as she began. "I love you, trust me."

Several moments later, Abby ran frantically from the lodge in a dire panic. "Lorella's hemorrhaging!" she screamed. "I can't stop the bleeding! We must get her to a doctor fast! Blaine, prepare a travois, while I tend to your sister. Hurry!"

# Chapter Fourteen

Blaine and Abby carefully placed Lorella on the horse-travois. "The nearest town is a tiny settlement called Callie Creek," Blaine told his mother. "But it's days away. Lorella will die first."

"Keep your voice down," Abby snapped. "Lorella must have hope. We must pray, son. I mean sincerely pray."

Hours of tension and arduous travel passed slowly.

"She's not moaning and thrashing," Blaine remarked.

"Thank God, she's unconscious," Abby said. "She can't be suffering any pain now."

Blaine pulled his horse to a halt and slid from his mount. Abby watched him walk over to the travois behind her and lift the blanket. He knelt over his sister.

"You're right about the last part. Lorella's dead!"

"Lorella has to be alive! You're mistaken." Abby jumped from her mount. She threw herself down upon the girl. Abby seized her under the arms, lifting her body. "Lorella's alive!" she cried. Abby screamed with all her might. "Lorella's alive!"

"No Mama, she's gone," Blaine said. "Lorella bled to death. We both knew it was likely to happen."

"No! Her life can't end here." Abby sobbed. "Lorella was my hope. If she could ever find happiness in this wretched, damned life, then her happiness was also mine. Don't you understand, son?"

"No, no, I don't."

Abby turned. She looked at Blaine, her face contorted. "You're responsible for this. If not for your vicious jealousy, Lorella would still be in Denver. Damn you, son. Damn you to hell!"

"Hey, I'm not the one with the bad aim on the darning needle. It was your blunder, not mine!"

Abby released Lorella and jumped to her feet. She raised her fist to strike Blaine. He caught her arm by the wrist, and bent it backwards. Abby winced in pain.

"I am no longer referred to as Ishkaynay. I am now Nahkahyen, remember." A fierce pride burned in his eyes.

"Can't you even muster a tear for your sister?"

Blaine said nothing.

Abby dropped to her knees. She buried her head in Lorella's bosom. "God gives with one hand and jabs you in the gut with the other," she muttered. "Once, I had faith. Still, He punished me. So it really doesn't matter." Abby's sobs turned to shrieks and wails.

"We've got to bury Lorella now," Blaine told his mother.

Briskly, Abby shook her head. "No, not way out here. Lorella shall be laid to rest in Denver."

"What? Why Denver, for god's sake?"

"We must do it," Abby was adamant. "Lorella was twice forced from Denver by society folks. Pompous fools! Well, she won't be driven out in death! We'll go on to Callie Creek to buy a coffin and buckboard for the journey."

"That's foolishness, Mama. We'll take her back and lay her to rest near Winnie and Noble."

"No, Blaine. It's important we do it my way, as much for me as for Lorella. Understand?

As they rode into the settlement of Callie Creek, Abby and Blaine remained in their wilderness attire. Lorella's body lay concealed by the blanket. The pair would allow no one close. They wasted no time in making the purchases. Blaine was anxious to depart.

Abby sniffed, and choked back her tears. "I need a shot of whiskey, son. I need one more than ever before. There's a saloon over yonder."

"You can't go in there, Mama. They'll throw you out. Maybe even arrest you for wearing men's clothes."

"At the Trading Post they took me for a man. Perhaps here they will too."

Abby carried herself with an exaggerated swagger down the dirt street. She paused beneath the huge sign of the Hunchback Saloon. Taking a deep breath, she entered.

As Abby approached the bar, a young whore with yellow curls, wearing a bright red boa and garters, winked in her direction. Abby's face tightened. She turned away.

The bartender, a large hunchback, stepped forward. "Callie Creek is away from the beaten path," he said.

"I ain't staying. Give me a whiskey."

"You're more than welcome to. My name is August, after the month of my birth, August Hanley." He offered his hand.

"I'm Ab…Abe Colter," Abby told him.

Half the day had passed. Blaine grew weary waiting for his mother. But he knew he dare not approach the saloon wearing Indian attire.

As dusk fell, Abby staggered back. She was in no condition to ride. However, Blaine was eager to leave. Abby was forced to lie in the back of the new buckboard, beside Lorella's coffin. When she wasn't throwing up over the side, she was passed-out.

The journey to Denver was a difficult, unpleasant one. Abby and Blaine quarreled bitterly and frequently. By the time they arrived in the city, they spoke little, if at all.

Abby forced Blaine to put aside his buckskins for more acceptable attire. His long hair was tucked up under a Stetson. Abby donned a dress, and hid her short-cropped hair beneath a ruffled bonnet.

Blaine looked himself over in the mirror and sneered.

"We must appear conventional," Abby insisted. "We're doing this for Lorella. Besides, you look far more handsome this way."

Blaine shook his head, and rolled his eyes in disgust.

The two found their way to the mortuary. The tall mortician condescendingly looked over the plain, pine coffin.

"That was just for transportation," Abby told him,

They were directed to the building next door.

"We're getting the best, something extraordinary," Abby said to the proprietor.

He gazed at the pair with disdain. "The best is costly. Perhaps the place across town would be more suitable."

"Is there something wrong with our money? Perhaps you should get a job across town." Abby bristled.

The man cleared his throat brusquely. He proceeded to show them his most expensive merchandise.

"This particular marker is top-of-the-line," he said. "Italian marble. Look at the finish."

"I want a mausoleum," Abby declared.

"What?" exclaimed Blaine.

"And I want statues, angels and cherubs. Also an iron fence and gate around the mausoleum. And don't forget, I need a new coffin."

"Mama," Blaine whispered through clenched teeth. "Let's go outside and talk."

Abby brushed him aside, as she stepped forward. "I'll settle for no less," she told the man.

"Indeed," he said dryly, as he added up numbers in a small notebook. "A monument of that sort would mount to around this figure." He showed them with a sly smirk.

Abby didn't balk. However, Blaine appeared flabbergasted.

"We'll return with cash for the plot, the mausoleum and the coffin. We'll pay for the ornamentations at a later date," she explained.

The proprietor did not seem pleased, but agreed to the terms. "And the name of the deceased, to be engraved?"

"Lorella Mae Two-Crows," Abby told him curtly.

"Did your common sense and ability to reason die right along with Lorella?" Blaine asked his mother as they departed the building. "You warned me not to turn Winnie's grave into a shrine. Well! That's exactly what you're doing with Lorella! How will we ever pay for an ostentatious tomb like that?"

Abby glanced at him impatiently. "First son, Lorella's kin. Winnie was not. And we have a sizable bit of money saved up."

"Not that much, Ma. You'll have us in debt for the remainder of our lives. And for what, a tomb!"

"We're just paying in part now, the rest gradual. We don't need the buckboard anymore. We can sell that."

Later, Abby was dismayed to learn their finances ran short, compared to the agreed upon price for the basics alone.

"I said so!" Blaine ranted. "You've never had a head for figures! And you're so muddled with grief, you're not using what little sense you've got!"

"Perhaps I can find something back at the lodge to sell," she intoned. "Did you bury anything of value with Winnie? Maybe something she brought from Europe? Try to recall, son."

Blaine looked at his mother in horror. At first he was speechless. "Never would I rob a grave! What has come of your sensibilities, Mama?"

"Lorella's our blood, son. She comes first."

"Lorella's dead, Mama! All this is unnecessary."

"I owe this to her, son. And so do you! Your sister's death brands us both with blame."

"Maybe Lorella owned something we could sell? Did you go through her valise? She must have brought back wages with her, after she left the Stricklands."

"It never occurred to me, son. I've yet the chance to go through her possessions. But your sister was only a governess. And that cowardly snake of fiancé even forced Lorella to give her engagement ring back."

"I suppose you believe that if Lorella can't live amongst affluence and luxury, she can at least enjoy her final rest in style."

"It's only fitting and proper."

Blaine shook his head and chuckled. "Lorella Mae Two-Crows! I can't believe you buried her with that name. Why? Lorella would puke in her shroud if she knew!"

"At least in death, show your sister some respect!"

"Yeah, like you showed respect for Winnie."

As soon as Abby talked the proprietor into another extension, she and Blaine departed for home. Once on the outskirts of the city, they cast off the conventional clothes for their usual attire.

"I'd like to stop at Callie Creek for a drink and a visit with my friend August Hanley and his regulars," Abby announced.

"That's out of our way. You can get drunk someplace else. Besides, you shouldn't be talking to strangers," Blaine admonished.

"They're not strangers. They're my friends and fine folk, too!"

"They think you're a man, Ma. They'd probably shoot you if they learned the truth now."

"We're going to Callie Creek," Abby was adamant.

Blaine waited with the horses on the outer limits of the small settlement while his mother enjoyed the convivial atmosphere of the saloon.

A rider galloped by on his way into Callie Creek. He did not appear to notice anyone else. A crumpled newspaper was tossed from his saddle. Bored, Blaine retrieved it.

Hours later, Abby staggered back. "I'll miss that place." She grinned wistfully.

Blaine shoved the newspaper into his mother's face. "This ought to sober you up for the ride home."

"What, what? My head is spinning."

"Look harder. You can at least see the photo, can't you? That's Ruben Jefferson Osbourne and his mother Vanessa. They're leaving on the overland stage to Wyoming territory in two days time. Going to purchase land and prime livestock there, it says."

Suddenly Abby turned almost solemn, and just as suddenly became discombobulated. "Got t'a rest, son, before we do more travel'n. Let me rest, sleep and think."

The following morning, she awoke ill, claiming to have suffered from nightmares the entire night.

"We've got to get home, Ma. No more delays," Blaine said.

"No, we're not going back just yet. We've business to attend. We've got to even the score for Lorella, so she can rest a little easier."

"You mean so you can rest easier," Blaine replied.

"Yes son, I suppose we're doing this as much for you and me as Lorella."

"Doing what?" Blaine was eager to know.

"We're going to intercept that stagecoach and give them exactly what they deserve. 'Vengeance is mine' sayeth the Lord. I used to repeat that phrase to myself so many times. However, God has a way of falling down on the job too often."

"Sounds as if you're planning to get us into trouble again."

"Trouble and grief is what life is all about for poor folk like us anyway. We'll need to use some of your Apache tactics to pull off my plan. I'll explain as we go."

As queasy as Abby felt from her hangover, she forced herself to ride, vowing not to take another shot of whiskey until Lorella had been avenged.

The two loaded up their Winchesters in wait for the Wyoming-bound stage. Blaine was attired in full Apache regalia, including bright war paint. He rode up ahead, toward several giant granite boulders. There, he concealed himself under a gray blanket sprinkled with dirt to blend in with the rocks. Abby remained hidden back down the path.

The rapid hoof-beats, jangle and clamor of the stage were soon heard. Abby watched it rock back and forth as the horses galloped by.

Up ahead, Blaine tossed off the blanket and immediately fired a warning shot as he darted in front of the startled horses.

Abby fired another shot as she raced up from behind. A loud, resounding gasp was heard from inside the coach.

"Stay calm, folks. Don't lose your heads," the driver shouted.

"Give us any trouble, or backsass, we'll blow those heads off!" Abby hollered. "Throw down your weapons! Everybody out, now!"

Vanessa Osbourne and her son Ruben were the first to step outside, followed by three nattily-dressed gentlemen, obviously of means.

Mrs. Osbourne was far more attractive than her photo. From a distance she appeared young enough to be Ruben's sister. However, she carried herself with the cool dignity of a mature lady.

Abby stepped over for a closer look. Mrs. Osbourne glowered back contemptuously. Abby spat abruptly into her face, before swinging around and shoving the rifle against Ruben's nose.

"Hand over your valuables, all of you!" she demanded.

The men eagerly did exactly as instructed. Suddenly Abby noticed the golden heirloom locket around Mrs. Osbourne's neck.

"You're holding out. That too!" Abby insisted. She poked the woman roughly in the bosom with her Winchester.

Ruben lunged at Abby to defend his mother. Blaine jumped between them. Without warning, Abby fired her rifle.

A man crouching behind the far side of the coach fell forward, killed with one shot. It was the wiry-built Shotgun; his Smith and Wesson had been cocked and aimed directly at Abby.

The passengers all palled, some shook.

Again, Abby shoved Mrs. Osbourne's breasts with her rifle. This time even harder. "Hand over the trinket," she snapped.

Reluctantly, the lady complied. "You vile, odious, little man," Vanessa muttered.

As Abby grabbed for the locket, Mrs. Osbourne deliberately let it drop from her fingers. Angered, Abby pushed her down. She kicked her and shoved her face in the dirt.

"Now pick it up and hand it to me, or I'll shoot you both in cold blood. Your son first!"

Again, Mrs. Osbourne reluctantly complied. Carefully, she handed the locket to Abby. Directly afterward, Vanessa arose and furiously slapped her across the face. "Trash," she rasped.

Seething, Abby punched her in the stomach so forcefully the woman dropped to her knees, writhing in pain.

"Savages! What sort of pusillanimous scum are you?!" Ruben shouted. "A defenseless lady, have you poltroons no shame?"

"Shut up!" Abby shrieked into his face. "Now throw down that strongbox!" she shouted to the driver.

Ruben raced to his mother's side as she clutched her stomach and moaned in agony.

"Tie them, except these two," Abby told Blaine. She turned her attention toward Ruben and Vanessa Osbourne. "Stand over here, so the others can watch. Now, you two, take off your clothes."

Vanessa looked horrified.

"I beg your pardon!" Ruben sniffed at the indignity.

"Strip!" Abby screeched. "Strip until you're naked as plucked turkeys. Do it, else I'll let Nahkahyen have his sport. You'll be tortured to death slowly, Apache style."

Vanessa gasped loudly, before swooning. Her son caught her as she fell backward.

Abby twisted open her canteen. She poured its contents over the lady's head, drenching her down to the chest.

"Don't faint again," she warned. "Otherwise you won't like the way I revive you next time. Now strip! Both of you, quickly!"

Embarrassed and hesitant, the mother and son did as instructed. The other gentlemen turned their heads, refusing to look. Blaine forced their gazes upon the pair, threatening to kill them if they glanced away, or even closed their eyes for more than a blink.

"You are depraved beasts!" Ruben seethed.

"Shut up, boy. Maybe you'd prefer to be dead," Abby replied.

Blaine rechecked the tightly-bound wrists of the men before herding them back inside the stagecoach. He and Abby looked the chagrined mother and son over. They laughed raucously as they ridiculed the two unmercifully.

"Those fancy frocks sure do hide a lot of flaws!" Abby guffawed.

"You're going to murder us, aren't you?" Mrs. Osbourne asked. She shivered more from fear than cold.

Abby shook her head. "After I've finished with you, you'll probably die from embarrassment. Nahkahyen! Bring me some of your war paint!" She called to Blaine.

Abby scrawled the word WHORE in vivid red across Vanessa's shoulder-blades and chest and the word FILTH across Ruben's. "See those two lead horses on the stagecoach? I want you each to mount one and then twist your pasty asses around facing me."

Frightened and confused, Vanessa and Ruben did as instructed. As the pair sat backwards, Abby and Blaine bound their captives' hands and feet securely to the harnesses.

"Now we're going to turn these horses back toward Denver. You're going home, where you're both well-known." Abby snickered.

She fired her Winchester high in the air. Blaine did likewise. With loud neighs the coach horses reared and bolted away down the path. Only a trail of dust followed Vanessa's shrill screams and Ruben's wails.

# Chapter Fifteen

Blaine said, "I thought we were just going to rob the Osbournes?"

"Those others were of the same ilk. Besides, now we can return to Denver, and do right by Lorella. She'll have the most elaborate tomb in the city, just like a queen," Abby told him.

"First, we'd better change our clothes right fast. Else we'll end up hanged. You killed a man, that shotgun over there, remember?"

"It was his own damn fault," Abby replied.

"Yeah, I suppose." Blaine sighed. "Vengeance sure satisfies and enlivens the soul. I didn't do it for Lorella. I did it for me." He grinned.

In fact Blaine felt so exhilarated by the experience, his mother was a bit disturbed. However, Abby was feeling too satisfied herself to fault him. With triumph, she fingered the golden locket in the palm of her hand.

"If you try to pawn or sell that, it's liable to be recognized and traced back to us," Blaine pointed out.

"This is going to be buried with Lorella. Vanessa Osbourne unjustly took it from her. Too bad we couldn't reclaim the engagement ring as well. Hey! Shoot the lock off the strongbox. Let's see what we've got."

To Abby's disappointment, the contents were mostly documents. She burned all those bearing the Osbourne signature.

Attired in conventional clothes, Abby and Blaine returned to Denver. The stage robbery was the talk of the city. The pair learned a large posse was already out scouring the territory for them.

"We'd better stay here awhile, as we are," Abby told her son.

Later, Abby finished paying for the cemetery plot, mausoleum, and coffin with enough left over for the gate, and one cherub. Still, it was not enough for her satisfaction.

"I want another cherub, and that angel over there. We'll be back to settle our account later."

Blaine shook his head in dismay as they headed toward the cemetery.

"Unseal the mausoleum," Abby told the undertaker. "I need to say good-bye to my daughter again. Son, you stay outside."

"With relief I will."

Three marble steps led down into the mausoleum's interior. At its center lay an ornately trimmed coffin. Abby covered her nose and mouth with a handkerchief as she lifted the lid. Moist tears dripped into the casket as she placed the locket upon Lorella's chest.

After another week in Denver, Abby and Blaine decided to risk leaving the city. Both were anxious to depart. Attired in her long, ruffled skirt and flowered bonnet, Abby waited outside the hotel for Blaine to bring the horses.

"Ma!" he shouted. "Look what I found tacked to the stable wall." He presented her with a Wanted Poster.

"Keep your voice down," Abby admonished. "Is that supposed to be us?" She studied the caricatures.

The drawing made Abby appear far more masculine and Blaine appeared a full-bloodied Indian; much older and savage in countenance.

"Everyone believes you're a man," Blaine guffawed. "But it's sure understandable."

"Ten thousand dollars on my head," Abby exclaimed. "Five thousand for the Indian accomplice, that's you."

"Well, you're the murderer, not me. We'd better avoid all the main trails home, especially after we discard these costumes. I'd like to make a bonfire out of these stiff duds."

"No, we may be needing them again soon. We've got more business to settle. Your sister has to be laid to rest proper before we return to the lodge."

"What do you mean?" Blaine was perplexed.

"We need more cash. Another stagecoach should do it."

"What? I thought we robbed that coach to even Lorella's score with the Osbournes?"

"It wasn't just the Osbournes that wronged us. It was all so-called decent folk. Remember, son?"

"We might get away with it once. But I don't want to push what little luck we've got."

"Just one more coach, I promise. We'll only rob them. We won't have sport with them unless they give us trouble, or backsass."

Blaine felt mixed emotions. He had no desire for a career as an outlaw. Yet, he had never felt more exuberant or in control as when they robbed that coach.

Abby selected a southbound stage out of Denver. The pair used the same technique as before. The passengers appeared less prosperous but equally terrified. Abby assured them no one would be harmed if they cooperated. This time more cash was found in the strongbox. Hardly a fortune, but enough.

"Well, at least one of those miserable bastards had something tucked away." Abby smiled and licked her lips.

Lorella's tomb, at last paid in full, became the most ostentatious one in Denver. Abby felt a sense of accomplishment.

"Now I can enjoy a drink to celebrate," she announced.

"We're not going to Callie Creek again." Blaine was adamant. "Whiskey might loosen your lips. You talked too much to August Hanley and his regulars as it was. That's dangerous, now."

"Maybe you're right." Abby sighed. "Miner's Bend is just beyond those woods. I'll stop there. Just one drink and I'll converse with no one."

As Abby stepped inside the saloon, she realized she could never limit herself to only one drink. Blaine knew it too, but said nothing.

As the bartender poured the first whiskey, Abby heard a raucous laugh behind her, followed by a disturbingly familiar voice. Abby turned, to her dismay she found herself staring directly at Jess Atkinhead.

He was grayer, but otherwise had changed little, still trim and muscular. Atkinhead was conversing with two other men. Several times he glanced in Abby's direction, but did not appear to recognize or even notice her.

Abby watched intently. She felt the blood surge and simmer through her veins, her flesh tighten.

"Something wrong?" the bartender asked.

"Ah, no, no," she nervously replied.

"Are you certain?" he persisted. "You seem ill."

"Just tend your bar. Don't meddle!" Abby shouted.

With those words, all conversation came to an abrupt halt, and all eyes curiously turned toward Abby, including Jess Atkinhead's. She gulped down her drink, then demanded another.

The trio proceeded toward the bar. Jess sat down with his back facing her.

An extremely pretty young whore with golden auburn curls came sashaying down the stairs. She smiled invitingly in Jess's direction.

As he tipped his hat, Abby arose. She stepped half-way between the bar and stairs. Jess stood to intercept the girl. Abby blocked him.

"You see something you fancy, eh?" She sneered.

"I believe the lady prefers me," Jess replied condescendingly. He extended his hand to the whore as he attempted to side-step Abby.

Abby thrust her foot in front of him. Jess flailed awkwardly and tripped. He stumbled face first onto the floor. Everyone, including the prostitute laughed uproariously, Abby loudest of all.

"You are one clumsy fool." She smirked down at him.

"You uncouth lout! You deliberately tripped me!" Jess quickly jumped to his feet. "I demand a public apology, or I'll have you thrown in jail. I'm Jessimyn Atkinhead!"

"You're a dung-gutted, spineless coward and liar, as well as a clumsy fool! That's who you are!" Abby screamed, almost spitting out the words. With that she flung her whiskey directly into his face.

"You puss-mouthed runt! I'm going to hammer nails into the sidewalk using your ugly head!" he snarled.

Jess took a swing at Abby and missed. She was too adroit on her feet. His two friends moved threateningly toward her. Abby pulled her six-shooter and cocked it. Everyone froze.

"So the little man is a big dude now with a gun." Jess sneered. "You could never stand up to me without that."

"I couldn't against three of you. It'll be a fair fight, unlike the last time. Just you and me. We've gone up against each before, Atkinhead."

Jess narrowed his eyes, trying blankly to recall. Abby ordered the other two men away with a wave of her gun.

"Step outside," she told Atkinhead with a shove.

Blaine was startled and dismayed to see Jess Atkinhead walk out of the saloon, ahead of his mother. As soon as he spied the drawn gun, he readied for a quick escape.

Abby directed Jess to the center of the town square.

"You've still got your firearm. This will be a fair draw, in spite of you." She holstered her six-shooter.

"What? Tell me who you are? I need to know before I kill you," Jess replied arrogantly.

"But Jess, you know me intimately," Abby told him in a breathy voice, little above a whisper."

Atkinhead appeared confused.

"If you try to cheat, which you probably will, Nahkahyen over there will shoot you dead." She pointed to Blaine, "He's a crack shot...you know the routine. We're going back-to-back until the count of ten. Then, we turn and fire until one of us is dead."

"Before we start, at least tell me you name?" he inquired over his shoulder.

"You know me intimately, Jess. Remember Lake Elisabeth?" Abby began counting out loud, stepping further away from him with each count. Fervid memories and emotions welled and surged inside of her.

At the count of ten, she whirled around and dropped to the dirt on her belly. Three rapid shots were fired from her gun. Jess fired two.

Abby swore she noticed an expression of recognition and disbelief upon his face before he fell. Two bullets hit their mark, one in his stomach, and one in his heart.

He died far too easily, Abby thought. He surely deserved to suffer.

Blaine raced up with the horses. His mother appeared numbed and dazed. He slapped her across the face with the bridle strap.

"Come on! Mount up!" he hollered. "Let's get!"

Abby jumped atop the snorting horse.

"Are you hit?" Blaine asked.

"No, he missed. But he recognized me before he died. I know that. I sent him to Hell."

The pair hid out amongst the thick mountain forests for days.

"I've been thinking," Blaine said. "Maybe we should go back into disguise for awhile. At least until we make it back to the lodge. We'll be safer that way."

"I was thinking that myself. It's a good thing I didn't allow you to burn those outfits. We're running short of supplies. We need to find a Post or a settlement."

"But no saloons, or whiskey, Mama."

"No, not this time, I promise."

Quickly, they changed their attire.

"You look silly astride a horse in that dress. Doesn't a proper lady ride side-saddle?"

"Hell, I don't know anymore," Abby retorted.

Three days later, they crossed paths with a trapper. He was on a mule going the opposite way. He directed them toward a Trading Post several miles to the east.

Outside the Post, stood a Federal Marshall with two lawmen. They were loading up supplies of their own.

"If we back away now, they'll be suspicious," Abby whispered to Blaine. "Remember, they're on the lookout for a man traveling with a full-blooded Indian."

As Abby made her purchases, she could not help but notice the Wanted Poster on the far wall. What she saw made her cringe. The drawing of her was a far more accurate likeness. Underneath was the name Abe Colter. In bold letters were printed the words, WANTED DEAD OR ALIVE.

Hastily, Abby motioned to her son. As Blaine distracted the clerk his mother ripped down the Poster. Quickly, she stuffed it down the front of her corset.

Without looking back, they rode swiftly from the Trading Post.

Later, she paced nervously back and forth before a campfire. "How did they learn that name?" she wondered aloud.

"Isn't Abe Colter the name you gave to August Hanley and his crowd?" Blaine reminded her.

"Yes, but August is my friend. And so are all the others at the Hunchback."

Blaine rolled his eyes. "What about Mary Peppertree's nephew? What's his name, Rutmore?"

"Jarvis Rutmore, and he only knows me as Colter."

"Then it had to be someone at the Hunchback Saloon. If not Hanley, then one of the others. Your price has gone up to fifteen thousand dollars now, remember?"

"Well, at least they still don't know any more about you, son."

"Yeah, well my price went up too. According to that poster, I'm now worth ten thousand. But I haven't told you the worst. While I was outside, I overheard these two lawmen. They said the Overland Stage Company brought in some Pinkerton detectives to track us down. Plus the Osbourne family has contracted a famous bounty hunter by the name of Ervin Bolthouse, from over in Dakota territory."

Abby shuddered. "I won't feel safe until we make it back to the lodge."

At long last, home was only a day's ride away. Both mother and son were relieved to be back on familiar territory.

"I'll never leave this area again," Blaine vowed.

"Doubt either of us will, now."

"As you recall, I never wanted to be uprooted the first time. It was damn bad luck." His voice bore a bitter edge. His eyes narrowed.

Abby said nothing as they continued on their way.

The two followed the mountain stream. Soon the lodge would be in sight. Blaine darted ahead. He grabbed the reins of his mother's horse.

"What! What's wrong?"

"Keep your voice down. I hear something, something damn unnatural."

Abby knew it wise to trust Blaine's instincts.

"I'm going ahead on foot. Stay here, and try not to even breathe."

As Abby waited behind, she heard a shout in the distance. Was it Blaine? She almost called out, but thought better of it. An hour seemed to pass.

Blaine suddenly emerged from the bushes up ahead. He motioned for her to keep silent.

"The lodge is surrounded," he whispered. "Also there's a Winchester waiting in a tree several yards from here and another behind the far ledge to the right."

"My God, they intend to kill us." Abby gasped.

"Keep your voice down, I said. We've got to get away from here, fast!"

Abby and Blaine quickly fled their home grounds. They rode at full speed, pausing only when their horses were ready to drop from exhaustion.

"We can't go back, ever. What are we going to do now?" Blaine demanded to know.

"We'll leave this damn country. We should be a whole lot safer down in Mexico."

"I don't want to live in Mexico," Blaine protested. "It ain't home."

"We have no choice, son. And we're going to need traveling money. We'll hit a stage or two along the way. We have no choice there either."

The pair ended up robbing four coaches in all, before arriving in New Mexico territory. During the third robbery, the strongbox booty yielded a small pouch, royal purple in color.

As Abby looked closer, she noticed the initials, O.C.L in golden embroidery. Inside the pouch were a gold and sapphire necklace, a large ruby ring, and diamond brooch.

"We'll pawn these across the border," she told Blaine.

In Santa Fe, they purchased a buckboard for the remainder of the journey. Eager to leave the country, the pair departed in early morning during a pounding rainstorm.

"Once down in old Mexico, we can discard these stuffy outfits for good," Abby assured her son.

About twenty miles out of town, one wheel became so deeply entrenched in mud, it appeared impossible to move. Blaine and Abby's efforts appeared futile.

"May I be of assistance, Ma'am?" offered a husky voice.

Abby looked up to see a big-boned, broad-shouldered man dressed in buckskins. Thunder boomed and lightning crashed overhead as rain continued to pour down in torrents. All were drenched to the marrow.

"Why, I do believe you were sent by angels." Abby smiled flirtatiously.

"There's a tree a'ways back. Let me hack off a branch. Perhaps that'll do the trick," the man said.

He rode off at a gallop, and returned shortly with a bent tree branch across his saddle. Mother and son watched as he placed one end firmly under the wheel.

"You!" He pointed at Blaine. "Pull these horses forward when I yell."

Blaine did as instructed. After three rigorous attempts, the wagon wheel rolled forth, free from its muddy hole.

"We're indeed grateful, mister, Let us pay you something for your trouble." Abby offered.

The big man shook his head. "I don't expect a reward just for being polite. But since we're headed the same direction, what do you say we travel together awhile?"

Blaine and Abby glanced at each other nervously.

"Where's your destination?" she asked.

"Ain't really sure." He shrugged. "I go wherever I can earn a dollar. Where you folks headed?"

"Texas, we're going down to Sweetwater, to live with kinfolk," Abby lied.

"Lordy, I could sure use a drink. You don't happen to have any spirits among your baggage, do you?"

"I sure do." Abby reached in the back of the buckboard and produced a bottle of whiskey.

Blaine appeared uncomfortable.

"My name is Abigail Crowe. This is my son, Blaine."

"He sure is a quiet lad." The man narrowed his eyes as he carefully looked Blaine over. "You got Indian blood, son?"

"His father was a half-breed Navajo," Abby quickly replied. She shot a glance at Blaine, warning him not to contradict her.

"A fine and misunderstood race, the Indian. We could learn much of value from the red man." He extended his hand in friendship. "The name is Bolthouse, Ervin Bolthouse."

The open bottle of whiskey dropped from Abby's shaky fingers into the ankle-deep mud.

# Chapter Sixteen

"I'm so sorry. What a waste of good spirits. I'm just plum tired. Please excuse me," Abby told him as she hurriedly retrieved the bottle. "There's a little spared in the bottom. Here, take it."

Bolthouse winked at her. He lifted the bottle to his lips and noisily finished off the remaining liquid.

"You may travel along for a'ways, Mr. Bolthouse. But after we break for camp and eat, I'd prefer you camped elsewhere for the night. It's only proper, you being a stranger."

"I understand, Mrs. Crowe. Obviously you were raised a lady."

Several hours later, they left the rain behind on their journey southward. The three stopped to make camp shortly before dusk. Bolthouse went out looking for game. Blaine promised to join him, but hesitated.

"Are you stupid?" he whispered to his mother through clenched teeth. "Why did you allow him to come? That's the bounty hunter from Dakota Territory! He's probably wise to us already."

"If he had recognized us, he'd have acted by now. Besides, had I turned him away, that would have raised his suspicions for sure. Think, Blaine."

"You coming, son?" Bolthouse hollered out from the woods.

Later Abby prepared roast rabbits seasoned with Apache spices. She and Blaine both kept a careful eye on the bounty hunter.

"So, Mr. Bolthouse, how long will we be enjoying your delightful company?" she wanted to know.

"My name is Ervin to friends, and especially to lovely ladies."

"Now don't you try flattering a chewed up, spit-out old thing like me."

"But you were a real head-turner once. I can always tell. Personally, I find a woman the most appealing when she's weathered, not a youngster anymore."

Abby chortled in amusement. "Then you're the opposite of most fellows. They figure if they get a gal young enough, they can train and control her. An older woman is set in her ways, also she's come to realize her own power. She won't put up with any guff or tomfoolery."

"I've always admired strength in a person's character, plus a challenge excites me. I'd like to accompany you all the way to Sweetwater, if you'd allow."

"Ah, well, my son and I aren't properly acquainted with you, Mr. Bolthouse, Ervin. What exactly do you do, to earn a dollar?" Abby hoped the nervousness didn't show in her voice.

"I'm a bounty hunter, ma'am. Does that make you uncomfortable?"

Abby took a deep breath. "Well yes, truthfully it does. My son and I are both Christians. We don't believe in stalking down fellow human beings for cash," she told him with false piety.

"I too, am a devout Christian, Abby. May I call you that?" he asked hopefully.

She swallowed deeply and nodded.

"I do our Lord's work, here on earth," he continued. "I hunt the predators to protect the lambs, as a diligent shepherd."

"You don't understand. I fear your presence will put our lives in danger, Ervin."

"That's unlikely. Besides, I'd never allow it. You needn't worry."

"Suppose your prey takes a pot shot at you and hits my mother instead?" Blaine interjected.

"When I find who I'm looking for, I promise to keep both of you out of danger, son."

"Don't you ever call me that again! Only one person here can claim me as son."

Bolthouse threw his hands in the air. "Geez! I'm sorry." He turned his attention toward Abby again. "You can use a man." He smiled.

"I have one. My son," she curtly reminded him.

"What I mean is, you need a man who's not kinfolk."

"Now don't you be telling me what I need, because you haven't an inkling, Mr. Bolthouse."

"At least allow me to accompany you both just a little ways more. I know I can be of help. Please, Abby?"

Again, not wanting to make Bolthouse suspicious, Abby reluctantly agreed, although she would have to continue to be extra careful to conceal her short, cropped locks and Blaine his long hair.

"Perhaps it's to our advantage," she whispered to Blaine later, after Bolthouse retired to his separate camp for the night. "We can track him this way. Maybe trick him into taking off in a different direction."

"Why bother? We should just kill him, first chance we get. Then we won't have to fret over him."

"No. We can't do that." Abby was adamant.

"But why? You've killed before."

"Those times were different. It wasn't in cold blood."

"Challenge him then. Like you did Jess Atkinhead. Make him enraged enough to want to kill you."

"That was personal, Blaine. This is not. You don't seem to understand the difference, son."

"But he's dangerous to us, Mama. He could bring us down anytime."

"You let me handle this my own way, hear?"

"Why you're smitten with that old buck, ain't you?"

"No, Blaine. You're wrong."

"I'm right, only you won't admit it. Probably not even to yourself. Remember, that sweet-talker would just as soon see us doing a jig on the end of a hangman's noose for his blood money. If he had any inkling who we were, he'd probably shoot us where we stood, armed or not."

"Son, you've got to trust me."

"The way Lorella did? Wonder if you'd entomb me inside a gaudy shrine as a reward for my trust."

Abby stiffened. "Once we reach old Mexico, you and I should part ways." She was seething. "Permanently."

"I've been waiting years for that, Ma. Finally I'll be the one who makes the decisions in my own life."

As the journey continued, Abby had to grudgingly admit to herself that she did indeed appreciate Bolthouse's company. However, Blaine remained jumpy and on guard around him.

The trio camped shortly before dusk. Blaine proceeded to build a fire. Bolthouse attended the horses as Abby unpacked supplies for the night.

"Once you're comfortably settled in Sweetwater, mind if I come by for a visit every now and then?" Bolthouse inquired hopefully.

Abby's fingers shook. She hesitated before answering. "We'll see." She reached for a faded blanket in the buckboard.

"This one is thicker," Bolthouse said. He reached for another in the back of the wagon.

Abby held her breath.

As he unfolded it, a small royal-purple pouch fell between them. Abby dashed to retrieve it. Bolthouse was swifter. He stood eyeing the golden O.C.L. embroidered initials in his hand.

"That belonged to my Aunt Ophelia," Abby quickly explained. She lunged toward the pouch.

Bolthouse adroitly pulled it from her reach. "My, my, and I thought the letters stood for Olivia Caulder Langsworth. Seems a pair of stage robbers filched a pouch exactly like this one from the lady."

Blaine reached for his six-shooter.

"I wouldn't, son." Bolthouse displayed a cocked Smith and Wesson aimed directly at him.

"How long have you known?" Abby inquired.

"I first suspected last night, right after supper. I was staring at this poster." With his free hand he reached inside his jacket. He tossed the paper at Abby. "I noticed your face in the firelight, and the resemblance. Still, I was uncertain. However, the other sketch looks almost nothing like the lad. He'd probably be safe without your company.

"I'm the one who killed, not my son. Ervin, let him go, please."

Bolthouse shook his head. "That wouldn't be right nor honorable of me."

"Hell! It wouldn't be profitable!" Blaine hollered.

The bounty hunter nodded in agreement. "I've a living to earn, son."

"Please, we'll give you the stolen cash and jewels," Abby persisted. "I'll tell everyone I spent or pawned them. I'll swear to it!" she promised. "Please, just let Blaine go."

Bolthouse seemed to be considering it. Abby appeared hopeful.

"No," he spoke at last. "I have my good name to consider. Besides, do you think you're the first desperados who attempted to bribe me?" He laughed. "All the time, so predictable, you thieves!"

"Now step over, close together." He motioned with his gun. "I'm going to tie you both up. Be grateful I'm fond of you. I'm going to take you in alive. I wouldn't be that benevolent to most."

"They're going to hang us. Ervin, please?" Abby pleaded.

Bolthouse reached inside the buckboard. He tossed her a rope. "Bind your son's hands. Tie them tight! Else I'll change my mind and kill you both here."

"Ervin, please?"

"I'm sorry, Abby. Now do as I said! No more talk!"

As Abby bound Blaine's hands, a coyote howled in a thicket nearby. As Boltouse swung himself around, he cursed.

Abby seized the opportunity to delve into Blaine's left boot. Quickly, she dropped something shiny into one of her front pockets.

With a rough push, Bolthouse shoved Blaine onto the grass. He seized Abby by the arm, attempting to force her down as well. She fought back.

"Do you want me to slug you?" Bolthouse sputtered. "Now, I'm going to tie your hands. Lie beside your son," he ordered.

Abby pulled herself free from his grasp. "Ervin, no. Take me alone. My son doesn't deserve hanging. Let Blaine escape. I'll do anything, please!"

Bolthouse seized her again, grappling her more viciously, attempting to force her down. "I'm sorry, Abby. I deeply regret this, I honestly do."

"So do I," she replied. Abby slipped her hand inside her front pocket. A brief glint flashed in the firelight. A half-second later the bounty hunter keeled over face first beside the supine Blaine. He was bleeding profusely, a hunting knife was lodged deep in his abdomen.

Abby pulled the lifeless body over on its back. She meticulously searched Bolthouse for cash and valuables.

"Hey, Ma! Untie me!" Blaine hollered.

"Just a second." Abby retrieved the pouch and pocketed Bolthouse's money. She dislodged the knife from his body and wiped the blade on the grass. "We'll bury him in an unmarked grave. No one will find him, at least not in our lifetime. Then we'll make camp elsewhere. I'm uncomfortable here."

At long last, Abby and son were visibly relieved as they crossed the border into old Mexico.

"No one knows this," Abby confessed to Blaine, "but I've been here before. Back when I was an Apache captive. I lived what seemed desperate, endless months in Mexico. The renegades escaped here after they raided our farm."

"I'm surprised you wanted to return, Ma."

"We had no choice. You know that."

"Did you learn any Spanish to aid us?" Blaine was eager to know.

"A bit, not much." Abby shrugged. "However, Chief Raging Storm and his tribe were fluent in the language. Seems this was part of their nomadic territory."

Blaine fingered the long fringe of his buckskins. "It sure feels fine to be rid of those stiff gringo duds."

The two traveled down to Mexico City. To their disappointment, they received far less than expected when they pawned the Langsworth jewels.

They ended up in a squalid and dusty little village called Caserio de Calma. Abby purchased a small farmstead. To her surprise, Blaine packed up his belongings and prepared to move on.

"I didn't mean what I said across the border," Abby told him, "about you and I going our separate ways, son."

"Well I did!" Blaine shouted.

"Blaine, you're the only kinfolk I've got now. I don't want to be alone. Please? I truly wish I had something more substantial to leave you besides this place."

"You might have, if not for losing your mind when you buried Lorella."

"We'll call a truce, son. Don't you ever throw Lorella between us again, and I'll never mention Winnie. They'll remain buried. You and I'll start fresh from here."

Blaine shook his head. "It's too late, Ma," he muttered. He hurried out the door never once glancing back.

Abby felt the tears streaming down her face. The idea of facing a future without Blaine seemed all of a sudden frightening and dismal. However, he was no longer a child and had made his choice.

The farm was small enough for Abby to manage herself. She remained physically strong and was accustomed to hard labor. Sometimes she imagined Blaine's presence close by. The thought caused her elation followed by sadness. She resisted the urge to find solace in a bottle.

After the passing of several uneventful winters, Abby had finally grown content in a life without him. Returning late one evening to prepare supper after a day of carpentry and butchering livestock, she was startled to discover a stranger waiting for her in the dark. Hastily, Abby pulled and cocked her six-gun.

"Ma! Put that away. It's me."

"Blaine!" Quickly, she lit a lantern. Her son appeared older, more manly. "What's wrong? Why are you here? You abandoned me, remember?"

"Every time I thought about you, I worried. Came back a few times and watched you from those hills over yonder. Don't know why. You're the toughest old turkey I've ever known."

"We have a bond you and I," Abby explained. "We've endured damnation together."

"There's a mud hut across the creek on this property. Thought I'd take up residence awhile."

"Blaine, not in a mud-hut. I can make room here."

"No, Ma, I need my freedom."

"Well, we can enjoy a meal together every now and then starting tonight."

Blaine was agreeable. The next day he began assisting his mother with the chores. Still, as the weeks passed there remained a secretive quiet about him that bothered Abby.

"Son, I feel like celebrating, now that you're here. Suppose we go to Saviero's Cantina in the village tonight for some supper and tequila?"

Blaine lowered his eyes and frowned. "I won't be responsible for you turning into a drunken sot again."

"Very well, then. Just victuals, no spirits."

Blaine appeared skeptical. Abby persisted until he agreed.

At the cantina, proprietor Saviero Quintana hastened to their table as soon as the pair seated themselves. Abby introduced him to her son. The graying, small, slightly-built Saviero was noticeably solicitous toward Abby.

"Does he know you're a woman?" Blaine whispered to his mother.

"How could he? I bluffed and duped them all just across the border."

At that moment the proprietor turned and gazed at her. His eyes gleamed as he licked his lip.

"Perhaps he possesses an instinct in that area." Blaine smirked.

"Or maybe he just prefers men," Abby retorted.

"Whichever way, the two of you can get together after I leave."

"What?"

"I'm going back to Colorado. My mind is set, Ma."

"Blaine, no!" Abby struggled to keep her voice down.

"Don't you realize how foolish and dangerous that is?"

"I may not stay. I just have to see it again, one final time. Colorado has been a state for several years. We didn't even know that," he told her incredulously. "It's home, Ma."

"You're not homesick, you're brainsick. Saviero, bring me a tequila!" Abby ordered.

Blaine grimaced and shook his head. "I'm leaving in two days time, Ma."

That night Abby was unable to sleep. Woeful and worried, and nauseous from tequila, she spent little time in bed. Abby realized Blaine would do as he damn well pleased, regardless of the risks.

As the first rays of dawn rose over the mountains Abby made her way across the creek to Blaine's mud-hut. He was outside washing his face in the water.

Abby took a deep, shaky breath. "I've been up all night thinking, son. Those overland stages we robbed were picayune when it came to profit. The real fortune lies in bank-robbery. We'll make our trip back worthwhile."

Blaine's back stiffened sharply, he jumped to his feet. "I thought we were all finished with that!" he expostulated. "You're coming, too?"

"One big heist, son, and we can have a hacienda overlooking the sea filled with servants. You'd have something substantial after I've passed on."

"You don't understand what I want, Ma. You never did."

"Wealth is freedom, son, freedom and power. No one would treat us like filth ever again."

"At least not to our faces," Blaine was quick to add.

"With enough wealth, we could live here as we choose, not as we are forced to now," Abby persisted. "That is the legacy I want to leave you."

"But we specialized in coaches," Blaine reminded her. "Banks are a completely different venture."

"Can't you comprehend? They won't expect us to rob one. That's to our advantage."

Reluctantly, Blaine agreed to the proposal.

"I'll sell the livestock and leave our homestead in the care of Saviero Quintana until we return. Let's hope he's as infatuated with me as you believe and he'll do us this favor."

Quintana agreed to Abby's request, but only for a reasonable fee.

"After we cross the border, we'll need to get back into costume again. I'm bringing a couple of sombreros and a few Mexican duds, too. Remember, bounty hunters and Pinkerton detectives await us like starving wolves. We're still wanted, dead or alive."

After crossing over the border into United States Territory, Abby and Blaine traveled the back paths and woods, often avoiding roads altogether. At one point, they were nearly robbed themselves when four men invited themselves into their campsite.

However, mother and son were better armed and more resourceful than the strangers had expected. Only warning shots were necessary to make the would-be robbers scatter.

Though it was well after midnight, the pair broke camp and continued on their way through the darkness. The following day, as they stopped to make camp early, Blaine paused to reflect upon their surroundings.

"We're in Colorado already. I can tell. I feel it."

"Perhaps," Abby said with disinterest. "Still, we have a ways to go before out final destination. We'll strike the most prosperous bank in Denver."

"That's not why I came back," Blaine replied.

"You once took delight in stage-robbery," his mother reminded him. "A bank won't be that different. Only our profit will be greater."

"Yes, I experienced fervor back then," Blaine admitted, "but I didn't like what happened afterward. I hated having to exist like a scared animal always on the run, always vigilant and cautious without knowing peace."

"We'll be safe again down in Mexico, only this time far richer," his mother assured him.

Blaine seemed skeptical.

After another arduous week of travel over back country, they came upon a hauntingly-familiar valley. Vacant, gaunt and ghostly-looking shanties of rotting wood were everywhere. A muddy, foul-smelling stream snaked its way among them.

Abby glanced at Blaine. "Remember this place? We prospected for gold in those dirty waters."

"I used to pray with all my might that you and I'd be the ones to strike the mother lode," Blaine recalled.

"You and me both, son. Remember Pastor Cooper, Tuck McCreedy, Brady and the rest?"

"Look! They even brought in the railroad to haul out all that gold."

However, the trains had long ceased to run. Trestles now rusted and rotted in the blazing hot sun. The lode had gone dry.

A sad sense of emptiness and waste filled mother and son as they rode the dismal length of the valley.

Abby began planning ahead to Denver. “We’ll scout the bank first; pretend to be making a deposit.”

“Denver is too big, too bustling. The peril is too great. We’d never escape,” Blaine pointed out. “Better to choose a smaller town.”

“The danger might be greater, but so would the profit,” his mother told him.

“Still, it’s better if we strike two small settlements,” Blaine insisted.

Abby thought it over, and figured Blaine’s reasoning was correct. They decided to rob a more sequestered bank. Blaine selected one near Pike’s Peak.

Abby, attired in a frilly, ruffled skirt and bonnet, opened an account there under a false name.

“There’s only one guard,” she told Blaine later. “But he’s a big man and he looks serious.”

“I’ll take care of him and the customers. You just collect the money,” Blaine said. “In the meantime, I found an old bear cave up in the hills. We can hide out there.”

# Chapter Seventeen

The day of the robbery felt lustrous and lucid. The air exuded excitement. Blaine displayed war-paint and Apache buckskins, his long hair unfettered. Abby could have passed for just another man.

She tied a red bandana over the lower part of her face, and then entered the bank first. Her six-gun raised and cocked, she fired into the air.

Blaine disarmed the guard. Demanding all weapons, he silenced the customers and staff. Abby ordered them to keep their arms high and in view.

She robbed the tellers first, then the waiting customers. Afterward, she ordered the clerk to open the back vault.

He refused, explaining he did not know the combination.

Abby placed her cocked pistol deep inside his ear. She threatened to pull the trigger if he refused again.

The frightened clerk pointed to a heavy-set, sharply dressed gentleman with a beard. "He knows!" the clerk insisted.

"You! Get over here!" Abby barked. She nudged the second gentleman in the direction of the vault with her six-shooter.

Nervously his fingers fumbled as the numbers clicked into place. The vault opened, revealing more cash, gold, and jewelry than expected.

Abby forced the man to shove everything into a large bank bag. She reached for it. The sack was so heavy, Abby had difficulty lifting it.

The bag tumbled to her feet as a gunshot rang out in the adjoining room. The guard had attempted a sudden jump on Blaine. Now the man was winged and bleeding.

Shouts came from outside. A customer had seized the opportunity for escape.

Abby hastily retrieved the sack. "Let's get out of here!" she hollered to her son. "Anyone who moves or tries to follow is going to die!" she warned the others.

As the pair raced outside and dashed for the horses, armed townsfolk started to close in from several directions. Gunshots were fired. Smoke, dust, confusion and resounding gunfire enveloped them.

Abby stumbled before reaching her horse. She felt an excruciating sensation in her abdomen, near her belly. Blood began seeping through her shirt.

Abby turned. The clerk she had first threatened was now holding a smoking rifle pointed directly at her. She fired back, and missed. Blaine helped her to her mount.

He fired rapid shots at the surging crowd. Frightened horses reared and scattered among the screams and gunfire.

Their horses charged at full speed as Abby and Blaine raced to safety. Vigilantes were close behind. Abby was growing weak. She noticed the bank bag was nearly saturated with blood. Blaine urged his mother on to their hideout.

After he carried her into the cave, Blaine led their horses inside as well. He concealed the entrance with pieces of scrub-brush and tree branches.

He wiped the war-paint from his face with a bandana. He then proceeded to tend to his mother before changing costume.

Later, when he determined it was safe, Blaine went outside to backtrack and conceal Abby's trail of blood. When he returned, his mother's condition had worsened and her pain intense.

"I'll help you into the lady-clothes, so I can take you to the doctor," Blaine told his mother."

"No." Abby groaned. "I'm going to die. You know it. I only wish I could have visited your sister's tomb again, just one more time. I thought I would."

Blaine lowered his eyes in anguish. He bit his lip.

"Listen, son. I've a plan for you."

Blaine sadly shook his head. He started turning away.

"No, wait! Hear me out. We'll make fools of them all." She took a deep breath. "I want you to turn in my body and collect the reward money."

"What? I can't believe you…."

"Blaine," she interrupted, "please listen. You'll have to return the bank bag with all its contents to be convincing."

"Also shear your hair, short as mine. You've got a heavy growth on your chin when you don't shave. You won't look as much an Indian. Glad I brought the sombrero and the Mexican duds. And you have a flair for

Spanish. Tell them you're name is Saviero Quintana and that you're a bounty hunter."

"It's another foolish scheme, Mama. It's doomed to fail, for certain. Everyone will be suspicious."

"Blaine, they're looking for an Indian, not a Mexican. As soon as you collect the reward money, disappear! Leave the country, fast! Promise me you will, please. If you don't you'll end up on a reservation at best, or hanged at worst. Promise me, son?"

Reluctantly, Blaine made a vow to his mother.

"When I was younger," Abby recalled, "I always tried so desperately to do what was right in God's eyes. Others cursed me for it. Now I could swear God and the Devil are actually one being, and we're all damned in the end." She forced a bitter laugh. "No matter what I've done, I feel entitled to a heaven, because I've walked barefoot through hell with my hands bound behind my back. Maybe St. Peter or a dead kin will sneak me in through a back window."

"Perhaps, Ma," Blaine said.

Abby's eyes softly closed. Her head fell to one side. Had she passed on already, or was she unconscious, or merely sleeping? Blaine wondered. He was hesitant to check.

Blaine sheared his hair almost to the bone. He burned the long, black tresses in the campfire. Abby moaned, opened her eyes.

"Put on those Mexican duds and saddle the horses. "We're going to the Federal Marshall's office in Denver, now," she insisted.

Dismayed, Blaine appeared incredulous.

"I'll be dead by the time we get there, son. So it really doesn't matter. It's just wasting time to delay."

He could see his mother was adamant. Blaine quickly costumed himself in Mexican attire. After the horses were saddled, Blaine lifted Abby onto her mount. She groaned in agony.

Blaine reached up to help her back down. Abby slapped his hands and kicked him away with a strength that surprised him.

"We're going to the Marshall's," she insisted.

As Blaine mounted his horse, he heard an unforgettable moan. He turned to see his mother falling onto the ground. Abby lay lifeless upon the grass, her eyes wide and vacant. Blaine jumped from his mount.

With both hands, he covered her eyelids, closing them. He sobbed as he lifted her into his arms. Blaine placed the body across the saddle, and then tied it securely in place. He wept for what seemed days.

The journey to Denver was filled with painfully haunting memories. At times his grief and anguish were nearly overwhelming. But thoughts of sorrow became permeated with anxiety as he neared his destination.

Blaine was tempted to just bury Abby, forget this foolish, insane plan and return to Mexico.

As he entered the city, townsfolk all paused to gawk, often with mouths wide agape as the strikingly handsome caballero rode past, leading a cadaver on horseback.

Reluctantly, Blaine was forced to pause and ask directions to the Federal Marshall's office. A group of men pointed the way, as one gave the address.

"Who was that sorry desperado?" another asked.

Blaine swallowed deeply. "Abe, Abe Colter," he said almost in a whisper.

"Abe Colter!" the man exclaimed. "That's Abe Colter!"

"This way to the Federal Marshall's office. Follow me, amigo," another hollered.

"Abe Colter, damn!" swore another. "I wanted to see that bastard hung! Imagine what he did to poor Mrs. Osbourne and her boy. Shaming and humiliating a woman and her son in that fashion. Such depravity!"

Others nodded in agreement, or shook their heads in disgust, or whispered among themselves, as a crowd began gathering.

"He deserved hanging!" shouted an old woman. "Why I'd a' brought my grandkids and packed a picnic lunch for the event!"

"Where's the Indian accomplice?" another man inquired.

"He got away," Blaine replied dryly.

The ever-gathering crowd followed Blaine to the Federal Marshall's office. Some led the way. Everyone appeared boisterous and excited.

After Blaine dismounted, he was forced to push his way through the curious crowd to reach the office. Some citizens were poking and prodding Abby's body. Others were spitting upon her.

Blaine spun around. "Hey! Stop that!" he demanded. He reached for his six-gun. The surprised crowd fell quiet. Everyone suddenly stepped a respectful distance away.

But after Blaine stepped inside the Federal Marshall's office, the crowd quickly resumed debasing Abby's lifeless remains.

"I've got the body of Abe Colter out there," Blaine announced to the Marshall and his staff. "And here's the stolen booty from the bank hit. I believe I'm entitled to fifteen-thousand dollars reward, am I not, senores?"

"You must have an outdated poster, amigo," the lawman informed him. "The Osbourne family has made it fifty-thousand. They wanted that wretched cuss with the wrath of Lucifer. What about the Indian?"

"I winged him but he escaped," Blaine lied.

"Well then, let's go have a look at Colter's corpse."

Outside the crowd had grown even larger. The Marshall and another lawman studiously examined Abby's body amid all the noise and confusion.

"That's him. Take the body to the mortuary," the Marshall ordered to his colleague. "You, amigo, come back inside."

The Marshall proceeded to count out fifty-thousand dollars in gold coins. Blaine tried to steady his hands as he collected the money. Nervously, he felt himself perspiring. He was eager and anxious to depart.

As Blaine turned, and walked self-consciously toward the door someone shouted out at him to stop.

"Stop him!" the voice thunderously repeated.

Blaine was tempted to bolt for the door. Realizing this was useless, he froze. Boldly he turned to confront them.

"There's also a twenty-thousand dollars reward for the stolen bank loot," he was told. "They never expected to see it again. Hope you're going to remain in Denver and spend your riches here, Senor."

"Quintana, Saviero Quintana. No, I'm not the type to settle anywhere," Blaine said. Fearing to take another breath, he departed with the currency.

Once outside, Blaine jumped upon his horse. He raced at full speed away from the area. At the same time, a startled mortician sent his apprentice scurrying to fetch the Federal Marshall, who hastened to the funeral parlor.

"What's wrong, Tom? Why are you so distraught?" the lawman asked.

Before he would answer, the undertaker directed his apprentice to another section of the mortuary.

"You must see for yourself, Marshall Waltham. Follow me, and lock the door behind us."

He led him inside an adjoining room. At its center stood a slab, upon which rested a nude corpse concealed beneath a sheet. The undertaker lifted the covering, revealing Abby's naked body.

"So, that's Abe Colter, ain't it?"

"Take a closer look, Marshall."

The lawman's mouth dropped open in dismay. His eyes grew wide, before squinting into slits, as he gazed in disbelief.

"I haven't filled out the official paperwork yet. I wasn't sure what to do," the undertaker confessed.

"It's best to keep this revelation just between us. Otherwise, it might prove too embarrassing to many other people. This shall remain our secret, understand?"

"Certainly, it shall go no farther."

"Imagine, Abe Colter a woman! Perhaps the Indian accomplice was a woman, too."

Meanwhile, Blaine had departed the city of Denver. He intended to keep his promise to his mother, and flee the country, but not back to Mexico.

After arriving in New York City, Blaine sent a letter to Salviero Quintana. The correspondence informed him that neither of the Colters would be returning; however it was their desire that Senor Quintana keep the property out of gratitude for his rare friendship.

Afterward, Blaine purchased a one-way passenger ticket. As he walked down toward the dock, a ship's whistle blew and smoke streamed from its stack. A young couple giggled and jested with each other as they strode ahead of him. The man glanced back with a merry smile on several occasions.

Blaine quickly turned away, avoiding eye contact.

As the ship pulled from its dock and headed out to sea, Blaine gazed wistfully over the rippling, wind-tossed ocean waters. An elderly gentleman suddenly appeared beside him by the railing.

"You look deep in deliberation, so serious for a young man," he said in an accent Blaine could not identify.

"I'm leaving everything I know, far behind."

"Then you're in for a truly memorable adventure that will alter you forever." By his countenance, the old man spoke from experience.

Not in the mood for conversation, Blaine turned away,

"What is your final destination?" the man persisted.

Blaine peered intensely across the seemingly endless waters. “I’ll decide after I’ve traveled the continent a bit,” he said at last.

“You shall be seduced by what lies before you, the grandeur of the Swiss Alps, the majesty of the Scottish Highlands.”

Inside Blaine began to ache, he thought of the foothills and mountains of Colorado.

“I am returning to my native soil, back in the old country,” the elderly gentleman told him.

“Someday so shall I,” Blaine whispered beneath his breath.

## The End

# About the Author

Dianne Lininger was born in Detroit, Michigan but raised in South Florida since the age of one. She currently resides in Vero Beach, Florida.

Several of Dianne's poems have been purchased by READ AMERICA!, an educational library publication.

Dianne wrote The Valley of Shadows and Shame in 1994. Writing and researching it helped keep her sane and grounded through a particularly horrendous period in her life. The manuscript remained in the back of a closet for well over a decade.

"I've always thought it was a good story and deserved to be published," says Dianne. "So in 2007 I blew the dust away, got a copyright and finally published it in 2008."

The Valley of Shadows and Shame is Dianne's second published book. Her first was the children's novel The Kingdom of Cydinah.

www.ingramcontent.com/pod-product-compliance
Lightning Source LLC
LaVergne TN
LVHW020627100826
845148LV00012B/2089

* 9 7 8 0 9 7 9 8 3 5 1 8 6 *